I0451299

Father Unknown

Deborah Wallace

Father Unknown

Published by Deborah Wallace

Copyright © 2020 by Deborah Wallace

Cover Art by Raymond and Deborah Wallace

All rights reserved.
This book is a work of fiction. All names, characters, places and incidents are either the product of the author's imagination or are used fictitiously. Any resemblance to actual persons, events or places is coincidental. No part of this book may be reproduced in any form by electronic or mechanical means, including information storage and retrieval systems, without written permission from the author, except for the use of brief quotations in a book review.

Chapter 1

Jasmine Kennedy opened her eyes and groaned, her head pounding with the same rhythm as her heart. She squeezed her head between her hands and sat up, not able to hold back a gasp. Maybe she should have waited to sit. The drapes hadn't been fully closed, and now she was out of the shadows with daylight searing her eyes. She slid one hand over them, then tipped it up like a visor, and peeked around the room. A hotel room. A closed suitcase sat on a chair, but it wasn't hers.

She should be in her bedroom at home. Her father's house. The memories returned, and she blinked back tears. Her father's funeral. Just yesterday. Her strong, vibrant father would never laugh again. Would never relish the first stages of finding a new, exciting company. Would never be there for her to lean on.

After the funeral, she'd needed to escape and found a hotel bar. She rarely went to bars, and never alone, but couldn't think of anywhere else to go where nobody knew her. Each time someone told her how sorry they were it made her cry. Even seeing how broken up her brother was made her cry. Watching other people meet up, talk, and laugh had helped to make life feel almost normal. She'd had a drink, or a few. She wasn't sure.

A glass clinked on the counter in the bathroom followed by the shower turning on. Her heart beat faster. There'd been a man, a sympathetic man, but she couldn't remember his face. Her gaze dropped to the suitcase. And they'd had sex.

At least, she was pretty sure they had. Flashes of hot kisses and more raced through her mind, and there was an unfamiliar ache between her legs.

All those times she'd had stuffy dates who wanted a pretty woman on his arm for charity or business dinners, and she'd turned down their offers of anything more. Now, she'd had sex for the first time—and couldn't remember any of it.

Whoever was in the bathroom, she couldn't look him in the eye, never having had a one-night-stand. What if he walked out of the bathroom naked? Sure, she must have seen him last night, and since she didn't have a stitch of clothing on, he'd seen her, too. It would be better if she didn't have to face any of it. Her black dress and bra were on the floor, and she frantically tugged them on. Her panties were nowhere in sight. There wasn't time to find them. She grabbed her purse, slipped on her shoes, and rushed to the door, closing it silently behind her.

In a corner of the lobby, she found the ladies' room, then washed her face and combed her hair. She couldn't remember the last time she had so many tangles. The dark hair had been in a neat bun for the funeral, but now hung to her shoulders. It would be fine. Not so much her dress. It didn't look like she'd slept in it, but it had a slew of wrinkles from spending the night in a heap on the floor. She untucked one side of the collar and smoothed it flat. Her hysterical laugh almost turned into a crying jag. Yeah, she'd slept naked, and from what little she remembered and how she felt, she hadn't slept much.

The laugh didn't help her head. Jasmine closed her eyes, and sucked in a deep breath. This should never have happened.

From the appearance of the lobby she'd flown through, she was in a large hotel. There should be a taxi waiting outside. She cracked the door open and peeked out. No one in sight. She tried to act like a woman on a mission and not a scared runaway.

Through the doors, the bright sunlight greeted her. She dipped her head and squinted. There. Two taxis. She got in the first one and gave her home address. Her brother would be frantic.

~~~

Nick Lawson felt great, wonderful, as he dried after his shower then wrapped the towel around his hips. If he hadn't been worried about waking Jasmine, he would have sung in the shower.

His meeting the day before had been difficult and he'd needed to unwind. He'd gone to the hotel bar, and seen Jasmine sitting alone at a table. He was drawn to her, but assumed she was waiting for someone. He ordered a drink at the bar and watched. She'd seemed sad, as if the world had dumped its worst on her. After ten minutes, he figured no one was coming. He'd asked the bartender to give him whatever the woman was drinking and brought it to her table, then asked to join her. Their gazes met, and he didn't know what he would have done if she'd refused.

It had been comfortable talking with her. She was intelligent and interesting, and her deep blue eyes drew him in. Every so often, they filled with pain, but he'd say something to distract her from it. He had a feeling she was at the bar to forget whatever bothered her. Despite that, she had told some funny stories and started laughing before the end. Spending that time with her had turned around his whole day.

He picked up his comb, and ran it through his hair. He'd been about to ask to see her again when she surprised him by asking if he was staying nearby and suggested they go to his room. He hadn't gotten that vibe from her until she'd asked.

She hadn't touched him or given him any indication that she wanted more than conversation.

She was beautiful and willing—and too hard to resist. His last girlfriend had broken up with him, what? Almost a year ago. She said he never had time for her. He'd plunged even more into building his business.

Jumping into bed with a woman he'd just met wasn't something he'd normally do, but the more time they'd talked, the more he'd felt a connection.

Maybe he should have resisted. But there was no way he could have known the woman who had thrown herself at him once they got to his room was a virgin. She'd peeled off her clothes, all except her little pink panties. He'd kissed his way from her lips down her body as he slid the last article of clothing down her legs. Her hands had roamed his body—his chest, his back and through his hair. She made the sweetest sounds of pleasure. Then she'd become insatiable, pulling him to the bed. He'd rushed through removing his clothes and rolling on a condom. Then there'd been the shock to both of them of her lost virginity, but she recovered first and kissed him.

He smiled. Yeah. He wanted more of her. The whole package. Now, he needed to get her phone number and find out where she lived. He came to New York once or twice a month and would love to get to know her better.

He strolled into the room and found the bed empty. He felt as if he'd been punched in the chest and couldn't drag in a breath. Her clothes and shoes were missing, as well, except for her tiny panties, which lay crumpled under the edge of the bed. He crushed them in his hand. The scent of Jasmine filled the room. A name as beautiful as the woman. He opened his suitcase and stuffed them into a pocket.

Maybe he'd scared her away or maybe she'd gotten what she wanted and didn't want any ties.

No woman in years had interested him the way she did. He needed to find her.

Chapter 2

Jasmine paced in her bedroom, cell phone in hand. She glanced down at it. Still four minutes to go. She didn't know how she'd been so... She shook her head. Once she'd left that hotel room two months ago, it hadn't crossed her mind that she might have gotten pregnant. Once she remembered her father, that's all she could think about. Her pain of losing him had wiped all other thoughts from her mind.

A month ago, she'd thought nothing of her period being light. The still numbing pain of her loss and Uncle Dean causing problems suggested stress and nothing more was the reason. Now though, she was a week late and no sign of a period.

She'd bought a home pregnancy test the day before and made sure Josh didn't see it. She knew what the results would show. She never expected to have a baby with no father. Not even a face for the father.

She'd had a wonderful childhood with two parents, but her child would have only her. Sure, there'd be Uncle Josh, but it wouldn't be the same. Eventually, it would be just the two of them. Her baby wouldn't lack for food, clothing or shelter, but that wasn't all they needed.

Her child was conceived three days after her father's death. He would have made a wonderful grandfather. She didn't bother wiping the tears from her cheeks. Her child wouldn't have a father, a grandfather, or the relatives on that other side of the family. All because of one pain filled day.

Beep beep beep.

Jasmine swiped the timer off and marched into the bathroom. She stared into the mirror at her tear ravaged face, too afraid to look at the test. She plucked a tissue from the box and dabbed at her cheeks.

She closed her eyes and pulled in a long breath, held it and let it out. Delaying wouldn't change the results. She opened her eyes and examined the test. Pregnant. Surprise. Not.

She planted her elbows on the counter and buried her eyes into her palms. This didn't happen to girls like her. Keeping away from the bad boys, dating the boring men so it was easy to refuse a second date. Then she went off the deep end and got pregnant her very first time.

A chill rippled up her spine. Sperm entered her body, what about STDs? She fumbled with her phone and found her doctor's number. She tapped her foot while waiting for the recorded message that told her if this was an emergency to hang up and dial 911, otherwise stay on the line.

For her, this was an emergency, but no one else would think so. Besides, nobody took an ambulance to get tested for infection.

"Barrington Health Associates. Good morning."

"Hi. This is Jasmine Kennedy. I … had unprotected sex. I just took a pregnancy test, and it was positive."

"Would you like to schedule a prenatal appointment?"

That wasn't the foremost thing in her mind when she called and she had to shift gears. "All right. But I need to get tested for STDs as soon as possible."

"You can come into our lab for a blood draw any time. I'll leave your name with them. They'll have results within forty-eight hours for some of the tests, but others will take about two weeks. Now, let's schedule your first appointment. How far along are you?"

"Two months."

"Can you make Thursday, next week at ten o'clock?"

"Yes. Thanks. And I'll be in this afternoon for the tests."

Her life had turned into one big disaster.

~~~

Jasmine sat across from Josh, and rubbed her temples. Her brother had been her rock, even as both their worlds fell apart. They'd continued breakfast together in the family dining room most mornings since their father's death three months ago. The first couple weeks had been painfully hard. Breakfast had always been a family meal, but the place at the head of the table now sat empty. No more conversations about who their father or Josh were meeting or the health of the various companies they owned.

Their mother had made the room homey with pictures of family outings and a couple of family portraits on the walls. The dining set was a replica of some kind of French antique. It could be expanded to seat twenty, but normally sat eight. Even ten years after her death, Jasmine could still feel her mother's presence in the room.

Three trays of food sat between them with clear lids, poached eggs, bacon and hash browns. A fourth tray held buttered toast.

Josh reached for the lid of the eggs, and Jasmine whipped up her hand and covered his just in time. "Don't open it."

He frowned and studied her. "Why not?"

She closed her eyes and shivered. "Because the smell of the eggs will make me throw up. I think I'll have to ask Lydia to not make them anymore." At least she wasn't having regular morning sickness. It was only certain foods that affected her. A few days before, she'd gone into the kitchen to talk to Lydia and the scent of raw beef had her racing for the bathroom.

He drew his hand back. "But I like eggs. *You* like eggs. Why would the smell bother you?"

She bit her lip, but stared resolutely at him. "I'm pregnant."

He sprang half from his chair before dropping back down. "Who? When?"

She drew in a long breath. She hadn't meant to tell her brother like this, but it didn't really matter. He had to know soon anyway. At least all the STD tests had come back negative and she wouldn't have to tell him about that fear. "When is easy. You know how I disappeared that night after Dad's funeral? That's when. But who? I don't know. I went to a bar and had a few drinks. A guy joined me. I remember only bits and pieces." Her face heated. Josh would know what that meant. Well, of course he would. She was pregnant.

"He forced you?" Anger filled her brother's voice, and he had no one to punch.

"No." At least, she hadn't felt like it. She'd always planned on being happy and married, giving her brother this kind of news. Now, she was confused and worried. No matter how hard she tried, no more memories from that evening came to her. She sort of felt bad for the man. He wouldn't know he was a father.

Josh squeezed her hand. "It's all right. You're not a destitute teenager with nowhere to turn. You've got me and enough money to be comfortable."

"Yeah. Twenty-three and more naïve than those teenagers. Thank you for being such a wonderful big brother. The money part, I'm not so sure about."

"Hey, we've both got our own money." He waved his

hand around. "And Dad's house. And we're going to stop Uncle Dean from stealing Dad's business."

"I know, I know. We've got the best lawyers. But that doesn't mean much if the board kicks us out when they meet in two weeks."

He squeezed her hand again. "That's not going to happen. They know we want to continue the company the same way Dad did. Uncle Dean has thirty years at Kennedy Holdings, but what he wants to do will tear it apart. The board will see that."

"I hope so." She wasn't as sure as her brother. He'd had four years of working with their dad, and she'd only had seven months. She'd worked as an admin in the summers, but she still lacked experience in the financial department. Josh had an understanding of how their dad worked, but the board had only seen their uncle's thirty years of working at the company. They didn't consider how often the brothers had clashed.

~~~

Nick glanced around the restaurant that Alex had chosen. Nick would have picked someplace quieter. TVs hung in all the corners, each displaying a different business program. He sat in a seat where he caught snatches of words from two channels.

Alex slapped him on the back. "I haven't seen you in weeks. I'm glad you called." He waved at the bartender and held up two fingers before sitting across from Nick. "Sorry the taxi didn't pan out."

"Me, too." He'd given the security man a couple hundred dollars so he could watch security footage of Jasmine leaving the hotel and getting into a cab, but he couldn't identify the cab company in the pictures. It was too frustrating. "My detective hasn't found anything, and I don't have any other ideas on finding her." If he'd had a selfie with her, the detective could have had something to go on. But the name Jasmine and a description hadn't been good enough, especially since he hadn't known if she lived in New York or was visiting. She'd been knowledgeable about the city, but it could have meant she visited frequently.

The waitress brought Alex's favorite dark beer and a refill of Nick's drink then took their orders.

Alex chuckled. "She must have made quite the impression since you're still so desperate after three months."

Nick rubbed the back of his neck. "Yeah." Three-and-a-half months, but he wouldn't say that. "Let's talk about why I called you." He had a hard enough time keeping his mind on business without the reminder.

Alex gulped half his glass and set it down. "So this is a business lunch? I figured you just wanted to get together since you were in the city."

"No, not business. Well, not my business. I want you to find me an apartment here." Alex was a realtor, and he ended up arranging more rentals than making sales.

Alex frowned. "Why? You don't come here often enough to make it cost effective."

The waitress stepped up with plates, setting a burger and fries in front of Nick, and a burger and potato salad in front of Alex. "Can I get you anything else?"

Nick glanced up at her with a half smile. "No, thanks." She hurried back to the bar.

"Why do you want an apartment?"

Nick took a bite of his sandwich, chewed, and prepared to be teased. Alex waited, drumming his fingers on the table.

"I want more time to find her."

Alex's glass was at his lips. He spewed beer and coughed. "Are you crazy? You do realize this isn't small town middle America, right? It's freakin' New York City, with a population of over eight million. And she might not even live here."

Nick shrugged. "Maybe." He tipped his head up and caught an image on the TV. He froze, eyes wide. A hoarse whisper left his throat. "Jasmine!"

He vaguely noticed heads at nearby tables turning toward him, but didn't care.

He focused on the picture as the newscaster relayed her story. "The Kennedy siblings have been ousted by the board of Kennedy Holdings, to be replaced by their uncle, Dean Kennedy. Dean worked closely with his brother for thirty-one years. Arthur Kennedy died unexpectedly in January, leaving the top levels of the company in chaos."

He barely heard Alex. "That's the woman you slept with?"

The scene cut to a live broadcast of the two young people. At the bottom of the screen scrolled, *Joshua Kennedy and sister, Jasmine Kennedy*. They ran down a set of steps. Tears streaked Jasmine's face.

A reporter yelled. "Mr. Kennedy, what are your plans now?"

Joshua stopped and took his sister's hand. "This isn't over. Our father built this company for his children. Uncle Dean was a big part of Kennedy Holdings, but it was never our father's intent for him to run it. Jasmine and I will not stop working to make sure our father's wishes are fulfilled." More questions were thrown at them, but Joshua wrapped an arm around Jasmine and shoved his way through the crowd.

Nick's breath left him in a whoosh. He'd found her. Odds had been so stacked against him that he wouldn't. His Jasmine was Jasmine Kennedy. He picked up his glass and drained it.

"Nick. Nick!"

A pain seared his shoulder, as Alex drew back with his fork in hand. "Ow! Why'd you do that?"

"Because you didn't hear me. Jasmine Kennedy is your mysterious one-night-stand?"

He glared at his friend. It may have been one night, but it was more than that. "Do you know anything about the Kennedys?"

"Just what's been going on in the news for the past few months."

"When did her dad die?" He grabbed his phone, and punched in a search for *obituary Arthur Kennedy*. He scanned the article. "Shit. It must have been a couple hours after the funeral when I found her. No wonder she looked so sad."

He had to see her, but her father's company had just been torn from her. Timing couldn't be worse. No worse than having her father die, and she'd ended up in his bed. He forced the thought away. He'd accidentally taken advantage of her before. He wouldn't do it again. This time, he would be a gentleman. She was worth it. No other woman had reached into him in just a few hours the way she had. Her ideals meshed with his. She made him laugh, even at himself. His heart didn't feel whole without her.

Nick pounded a finger on the table. "I want that apartment yesterday. A lease that's fully furnished would be ideal."

Alex grimaced. "Yeah, sure." He raised his arms. "You know how hard that's going to be to find?"

Nick leaned forward. "Pull some strings."

Chapter 3

Jasmine had to hold herself together, at least until they got home. She snatched a tissue from the box on the seat beside her and dabbed at her face. It was a good thing Josh had ordered the limo. She wouldn't have wanted to wait on the curb for a cab while reporters shouted questions.

Slow breath in. Slow breath out. Repeat. By the time the limo pulled into their circular drive at home, and Josh helped her from the car, she was almost back to normal. Almost.

As soon as Josh closed the door behind them, she burst into tears. "Josh, how could Uncle Dean do this to us?"

He hugged her tight. He was as upset as her, but he covered it better. "We'll get it back. You'll see."

She squeezed him harder. "I'm sorry I'm falling apart. I feel like I can't do anything to help you."

He tipped his head to the side and stared at her. "I think I read somewhere pregnancy hormones can make a woman emotional. I'll make allowances, since normally you're pretty tough. We'll come up with something together."

She nodded. Her brother had been unbelievably understanding. "I'm exhausted. Do you think we can come up with it tomorrow?"

He chuckled. "That's fine. Go rest. And if you're not awake by dinner time, I'll come get you." He turned her around and nudged her in the direction of the stairs.

She trudged up them, sat on the bed and fell back, only then kicking off her shoes. She rolled and stared at the ceiling.

Her life had spun out of control. She caressed her stomach. Her childhood had been wonderful with a loving father, and she was saddened her own child wouldn't know that kind of love. For now, Josh could fill that role, but he'd get married some day and have his own children, and then she'd be alone to raise a child.

She rubbed her sleeve across the new tears. Stupid pregnancy hormones.

~~~

Nick straightened his bow tie and grimaced. A tux. A charity ball. Not something he ever expected to attend. It had been over two weeks since he found out who Jasmine was, and he'd been assured she would be at this event. Her family had attended the children's hospital ball for the past ten years, but that was before her father died and his company was stolen from her.

No matter. It was worth the thousand dollars it had cost for a ticket. Even if she wasn't there, he might glean more information about her.

He peeked into the living room. "Hey, Alex, don't wait up for me."

Alex glanced up from his laptop, and gave him a lazy salute. "Good luck."

"Thanks."

Alex was the best friend a guy could have. He'd invited Nick to stay with him until his apartment became available. That was a week ago, and he still had two more to go before he could move in. In college, they'd spent many school breaks at each other's homes.

Nick took the elevator down fourteen floors to the lobby. The cab he'd called waited out front. He opened the back door. "Hi. Are you the one taking me to The Palace?"

The driver nodded. "That would be me."

Nick slid into the seat, and rubbed his sweaty palms on his pants. His stomach tensed and he wondered if he'd be able to eat. Maybe he'd spend the whole evening wandering around and never find her, or she wouldn't talk to him.

They stopped in front of the hotel, and Nick drew in a deep breath. He paid the driver and joined the stream of people headed to the hotel lobby. The line moved at a fast pace.

He stopped in front of the woman with a clipboard and pen, and handed her his ticket. "Nick Lawson."

She scanned her list and checked his name off, then smiled up at him. "Is this your first time at our ball, Mr. Lawson?"

"Yes, but hopefully, it won't be my last." If it worked out with Jasmine, he wanted to have her on his arm as they strolled into this event next year.

She smiled. "Yes, hopefully. Have a good evening."

He stepped into the room and scanned the crowd. The women wore beautiful dresses in every color. The men were dressed like him in black tuxes—almost like a uniform.

The floor was covered in a patterned carpet too hard to distinguish in the milling crowd. The walls were tan, trimmed with white molding. Multi-tiered chandeliers hung from the high ceiling, giving the room a golden glow.

Nick grabbed a drink from a passing waiter and wandered the room. He recognized some faces he'd only seen on TV.

A woman stepped into his path, and he stopped inches from her. His drink spilled over his fingers, barely avoiding the front of her royal blue sheath. Her eyes matched the color of her dress, which contrasted with the dark curls piled on her head. She ran a finger down his shirt until it was stopped by his jacket. "Hi. I'm Steph. I haven't seen you at one of these before."

"It's my first one."

She pressed against him. "I can keep you company, make introductions."

He stepped back. "No thanks. I'm looking for someone." She was beautiful, in a cold sort of way. At one time he might have taken her up on her offer, knowing where they'd end up. But now, he wanted to find the warm woman he couldn't forget.

He sidestepped and almost chuckled at her pout. He continued around the room, scanning every woman's face, not finding the one he sought.

The crowd hushed, and he turned to where all eyes were riveted. Then he forgot to breathe. *Jasmine.* Her wine-colored dress nearly touched the floor. It gathered at one side of her waist, and beaded flower petals ringed the neck and cap sleeves. Sheer fabric draped the narrow skirt. Her glossy, dark hair swept up with a few strands loose at her ears. His fingers itched to pull out the pins and run his hands through it the way he had months ago.

Even halfway across the room, her nervousness was evident. Probably everyone knew what had happened to her father's company and it set her on edge. He wished he could help ease her discomfort.

Joshua whispered in her ear, and she gave an almost imperceptible nod. She lifted her chin, and they entered the room.

She was more beautiful than the teary version on the TV screen or when he'd found her alone and sad in the bar. This aloof vision competed with the enchantress who had shared his bed.

He found himself gravitating toward her, but stopped as she swept past without making eye contact.

Maybe she was too nervous to look around, or maybe she'd seen him and ignored him. She might be embarrassed at what they'd done together. He needed to talk to her.

~~~

Jasmine tried to relax her grip on Josh's arm, but she hadn't expected to be the center of attention when they arrived. "I need food now." Sometimes she couldn't eat at all, and others, food was the only thing she could think about. At three-and-a-half months, she'd thought symptoms would smooth out. She shifted closer to her brother. "I hate all these pregnancy symptoms."

Josh patted her hand. She couldn't ask for a more supportive brother, even as he'd lost their father right along with her. The company was taken from him, but he didn't waver from her side. He stayed strong for her, even when she'd dropped one more disaster in their laps. She touched her stomach. This baby would not be a disaster.

They stopped in front of the hors d'oeuvre table, and she snatched up a plate. She'd added three delectable items to it when an odor stopped her, and she took a step back. "Um, Josh, can you get me one of those crab rolls beside the deviled eggs?"

He chuckled and stepped back to her. "They really do bother you, don't they?"

"That's why you have to eat eggs in the kitchen."

"At least Lydia doesn't mind when I eat in there. I thought maybe it was a morning thing. He took her plate from her."

She leaned closer. "No. I think it's a pregnancy thing. The smell of them makes me feel sick."

He nodded toward an area of small tables surrounded by chairs. "Why don't you have a seat, and I'll finish filling this?"

"Thanks." She hurried to a table and sat. Getting away from the stares and off her feet, she already felt better. She closed her eyes and drew in some air. Josh sat down beside her. She opened her eyes. "Tha…"

It wasn't Josh, but a stranger. A really breathtaking stranger. His shoulders filled out his tux better than most men's. Dark hair and curls. Just long enough to tell he had curls, but not so long it was unruly. Dark, dark brown eyes she could get lost in. A straight nose, and lips she imagined kissing. Her lips tingled and she almost reached up to touch them.

"Jasmine—"

"Who are you?" She covered her mouth. "Sorry. That was rude, but I'm famished and grouchy." Yeah, stupid low blood sugar making her crabby.

He frowned, then smiled, holding his hand out. "I'm Nick Lawson. I had to introduce myself to the most beautiful woman here."

His smooth voice wrapped around her like a comfortable sweater. She scanned the room. "I'm not the most beautiful." She took his hand, and a tingle zipped up her arm.

"To me, you are." His expressive eyes made her think he meant it.

He released her hand, and she felt like a part of her had gone with it. He seemed sort of familiar. Maybe she'd seen him somewhere. He was definitely worth looking at. And kind. Somehow, she knew he was compassionate.

Josh set her plate before her and dropped into the chair on her other side. Jasmine's dish held twice as much food as his.

Josh eyed the stranger. "Josh Kennedy. And you are?"

She loved how protective Josh was.

He held his hand out to Josh. "Nick Lawson."

Josh studied the man for several seconds, then shook his hand. "What business are you in?"

"I own a growing cyber security company, Lawson Prime Secure. I'm in the process of moving my main office to New York."

Nick's voice caused her heart to flutter. No man's voice had ever had that effect before, not even singers of sexy love songs. She imagined him whispering something naughty in her ear, and her face warmed. Oh, please don't let him notice.

"Why the move?"

"Minnesota isn't exactly the center of the business world, and I've been traveling to New York more often." He stared into her eyes. "Or maybe it's because this is where Jasmine is."

Josh snorted.

Jasmine's mouth became the Sahara Desert. She couldn't take her eyes off him. It made no sense, but for this instant, she believed he meant it.

Nick stood. "If you'll excuse me, I'll leave you to your appetizers."

He strode away, and she almost wanted to run after him.

Josh brought her attention back to him. "Did it work? Maybe I should try a variation of that 'because you're here' line."

"Yeah, it worked." She searched where she'd last seen him, but he'd disappeared.

She nibbled on the appetizers until it was time to go in to dinner.

Josh found their seats near the stage. If it wasn't the same table as the year before, it was close. Her father's place card sat at the next table setting and she flipped the card down. The organizers should have removed his name from the list.

A stick with a number sat beside each place, reminding her of the auction. "I wish you'd been able to remove me from the auction list."

Josh squeezed her hand. "Sorry, sis. All the lists were printed by the time I asked. I *did* have them change your introduction. Besides, you did it last year, and it turned out fine."

She sighed. "Yeah, but last year, I was the daughter of a successful business owner. Now, I'm practically impoverished. I'm afraid I'll stand up there and no one will bid to have dinner with me."

Josh leaned closer to his sister, and scowled. "Hey, enough with the self-pity. You're beautiful, and everybody you meet likes you." He smirked. "And if nobody bids after five or ten seconds, I'll make a bid."

She bumped her shoulder against him. "Just what I want. A date with my brother."

The director of the children's hospital foundation, Jonathan Ambrose, walked across the stage and turned on the mike with a click. He droned on as Jasmine's mind returned to the handsome stranger named Nick, and desperately hoped she'd see him again.

Chapter 4

Nick found his seat near the back of the room, and introduced himself to the others already at the table. He picked up a stick with the number two hundred twenty-two on it. "What's this for?"

The woman next to him touched his arm. "You don't know? That's for the auction. Twelve women are being auctioned off for dinner dates."

"What? They're auctioning women?" He might have seen it on a movie, but didn't think it was something done in real life.

She laughed. "One dinner at the dining room in this hotel. This year, three men are being auctioned, too." She leaned closer. "I'm on the list. Will you bid on me?"

She was a pretty girl, but forthright. "Sorry, I already have a woman in my life." He'd try his hardest to make it true, even if Jasmine didn't remember their night together, which had shocked him. She'd shown no sign of recognition. He didn't know how much she'd had to drink before he joined her, but he never realized she'd been so far gone. It would probably work out better this way, getting to know each other before becoming intimate again. He thought he'd find her and immediately ask her out. He'd have to rethink the best way to get her to say yes.

He shared a lively conversation through dinner with

those around him and then the children's hospital director returned to the stage. "Now, the moment everyone's been waiting for. I'd like the young ladies and gentlemen who will be our dinner auctions to come up. Last year, this portion of our fundraising netted over twenty-two thousand dollars. We have five more participants this year, so let's hope we beat that record."

The woman to his right stood and made her way to the front. As the first woman ascended the stairs, the director pointed to the chairs on his right.

Nick fumbled his drink, nearly spilling it. His dream had come true. Jasmine was one of the women, and whatever it cost, she was going to dinner with him. He could barely contain his excitement, now that he had a guarantee they'd spend time together. Fate had given him a shortcut.

"Did you change your mind about bidding on Samantha?" The woman on his left must have noticed his reaction.

"No. The woman I'm going to date is up there. It was unexpected."

"I thought you said you've got a woman in your life."

"It's complicated." He concentrated on the front, not wanting to miss anything important.

After the men and women being auctioned were seated on the dais, the director turned back to the audience. "You'll be bidding on a dinner with one of the women or men behind me. It will take place in the hotel dining room within the next three weeks, on an evening agreed upon between the two parties. Dinner for two and wine will be provided. Winners, please remain on the stage until all auctions are completed. After all bidding is complete, winners, bring your number with you when you claim your prize."

Nick stared at Jasmine, willing her to turn her gaze on him. She caught her bottom lip between her teeth, and her hands clenched in her lap. He wished he could tell her she had nothing to fear.

Ambrose lifted a card. "First up, Amber Newton. Her father, Clark Newton, is head of surgery at Children's. She is currently in the residency program at the same hospital."

Amber walked to the podium, stood beside Ambrose, and smiled at the audience.

"Bidding begins at two hundred dollars."

A number card was thrust up. "Two hundred."

Another man called out. "Four hundred."

Bidding progressed among three bidders for a time, until one remained at eighteen hundred dollars.

The director pointed to the man with the final bid. "You are the winner, number forty-seven. What's the name?"

"Lucas Thayer." The blond man sent a kiss to Amber before leaning back in his seat.

The director wrote on the card and handed it to Amber. She returned to her seat on the stage.

"Next up is Jennifer Watson."

Nick checked his watch. If it took the same amount of time for bidding on each person, it would be at least an hour and a half before it was done, and he didn't know where Jasmine was in the lineup. He sat back, rocked his head side to side, and loosened his shoulders. It was an unexpected bonus to bid on a meal with Jasmine. This was even better than the plan to convince her later to go on a date with him. Now, he'd get that date without trying and had a chance for her to get to know him.

As the bidding closed for each participant, Nick leaned forward, ready to grab his number. Bidding had been completed on six women and two men.

"Next up, Jasmine Kennedy."

Nick snatched up his number.

His tablemate's eyes widened. "It's Jasmine you want a

date with?"

He turned his gaze to the front. "Yes."

The director read from his card as she strolled across the stage to stand beside him. She didn't smile like the other auctionees. "Daughter of the late Arthur Kennedy, Jasmine graduated *summa cum laude* from Columbia University with a bachelor's in economics. She volunteers in an after school program for high schoolers interested in starting their own business. Bidding shall begin at two hundred."

Nick and two other men raised their numbers and simultaneously said, "Two hundred."

Jasmine's gaze bounced between the three, and maybe it was wishful thinking, but he thought she'd looked at him the longest.

Nick raised his stick higher. "Four hundred."

One of the men said, "Five hundred," while the other called out, "Six hundred."

The first man set his number back on the table.

Nick held his number higher. "Eight hundred." He wouldn't stop until he'd won.

The two continued in two hundred dollar increments, the other man's responses slower as the number increased.

Jasmine bit her lip again. He hoped it wasn't because she didn't want him to win.

Nick punched his number up. "Two thousand."

The man glanced back at Nick and glared. Yeah, Nick was in the cheap seats. The man hadn't expected the competition from behind him. "Twenty-two hundred."

Nick was done fooling around. He hoisted his number again. "Three thousand."

A pause. "Three thousand going once..." Ambrose called out.

The other man raised his number. "Thirty-two hundred."

Nick snapped his card up. "Thirty-five hundred."

Another pause. "Thirty-five hundred going once…going twice…sold to number two-two-two. Name?"

Nick stood and grinned at Jasmine. "Nick Lawson." The man who lost to him glared, and he was so glad he'd saved Jasmine from that guy.

Ambrose wrote on the card and handed it to Jasmine. She smiled at Nick before returning to her seat. He hoped that meant she was glad he was the winner.

He dropped into his chair and set his number on the table. Nick was pretty sure he had a silly grin on his face.

The man to his left leaned around his girlfriend. "You look like the cat that got the golden canary. You go all out when you make up your mind."

Nick sobered. He didn't want Jasmine to see him as overly eager, and scare her. "In this case I do. And next year, she won't be on the auction block."

He sat back, and relaxed as he waited through the rest of the bidding, glad that Jasmine hadn't been last.

Ambrose smiled at the audience. "Thank you, ladies and gentlemen. I'm pleased to announce tonight's auction will net 35,200 dollars. Now, if the winners will form a line at the first table, we'll try to finish up quickly."

Being in the back, Nick was the last person in line. He kept an eye on Jasmine. She looked tired. Josh joined her and held her hand.

He made his payment, then climbed the stairs to join Jasmine, sitting beside her.

"You didn't have to do that." A crease marred the spot between her eyebrows.

He widened his eyes. "You wanted a date with that other guy?"

She smiled. "No. But that's a lot of money."

He shrugged. "It's for charity. Will you go on this date with me?" It couldn't hurt to ask since she almost had to say yes.

She laughed and tugged a phone out of a tiny purse. "Yes. What day do you want to do this?"

"I can make any day you choose work."

Jasmine scrolled her phone, and a calendar popped up. "How about this coming Wednesday?"

He wished she showed some excitement, but he was a stranger to her. He'd have an evening to convince her to see him again.

"Perfect. Shall I pick you up?"

Her tired eyes were still a beautiful blue. "How about if we meet in the lobby at six-twenty then you can see me home afterward?"

It would have been nice to spend more time with her, but the stress of the evening seemed to have taken a toll. One more touch would have to get him through until he saw her again. Her hand was small in his with one of his fingers resting on her wrist. Her pulse quickened. "See you Wednesday, beautiful Jasmine. Pleasant dreams." He hoped she dreamed of him, as he had of her so many nights. He released her hand and stood.

Josh stepped close to him and spoke in a harsh whisper. "I'll be sure to find out how this date goes."

"It's admirable how much you look out for your sister." He'd try his hardest to make friends with Josh. He didn't want Jasmine at some point to feel like she had to choose.

Jasmine stood and swayed until Josh put his arm around her. "Bye, Nick."

His Jasmine. One step closer.

~~~

Jasmine stared at the four rejected dresses on the bed, then glanced at herself in the mirror. This fifth one would

27

have to do. At least she wasn't noticeably pregnant in it, like the two slinky dresses she'd tried on. Or like a kid in the third one. That one must have been stuck in the back of her closet for a while. The fourth seemed more fitting for a formal wedding.

A slow spin in front of the mirror showed her the dress from all angles. The deep blue matched her eyes, and the empire waist and flared skirt hid what she wanted hidden. It stopped two inches above her knees, and showed more cleavage than the last time she'd worn it, but she was bigger on top now.

She'd left her hair down and curled it, so it looked fuller. It made her appear younger than her twenty-three years. Hopefully, that wasn't a bad thing.

Jasmine smoothed concealer under her eyes and added some blush, lengthened her lashes with mascara, then swiped on a deep pink lipstick.

One last check of the entire package, she decided it would do. This was the fourth time she'd had an auction date. Two of the other men had asked her out again, and she'd refused. If Nick didn't asked her, she might break her rule and ask him first, despite having to tell him about the baby soon.

Downstairs, she stood in the living room doorway. Josh watched a sporting event. Cheers erupted from the TV.

He glanced up. "You ready?"

"Yes. You know I can take a cab."

"Not happening. I'm dropping you off. And I'd pick you up, too, if you'd let me."

"Not happening." She smiled as she repeated his favorite phrase.

He took her hand. "Okay. But if he turns out to be a complete douche and you need a ride, call me."

She stood on her toes and kissed his cheek. "Thank you.

You're a better brother than I deserve."

He grinned. "Hey, you deserve the best, and you got it."

He hit the remote and turned the TV off. "Let's go."

They approached the hotel, and Jasmine's hands trembled. Last year, her auction date had been handsome but boring. He'd talked about his successful business too much. Maybe he'd thought he had to compete with her father's company. A cramp in her heart reminded her that wouldn't be an issue this year.

She took a deep breath, and it eased the tightness in her chest. She could do this. One date. With a man she found more attractive than any other.

Josh stopped in front of The Palace Hotel, and placed his hand on her arm. "You're sure about this?" He narrowed his eyes. "There's something about him that seems too eager."

"Yes, Josh. I'm sure. He paid thirty-five hundred dollars for this dinner. I can't back out." Besides, she wanted to have dinner with Nick.

Jasmine stepped into the lobby at six twenty-one. Her eyes were immediately drawn to Nick Lawson as he catapulted out of a chair and hurried toward her.

He took her hands in his and kissed her cheek. She hadn't expected that. If the man who won the bid last year had done it, she would have been repulsed, but with Nick, it was different. She almost wished she'd been prepared for it and turned her head so their lips could touch.

His eyes gleamed. "You're beautiful. I love your hair down."

"Thank you." She hoped he didn't notice the heat creeping up her neck and into her face.

"Let's get seated." He took her hand and led her to the restaurant and up to the hostess. "Nick Lawson and Jasmine Kennedy."

The hostess greeted them with a wide smile. "Ah, one of

the auction winners. Your table is this way." She picked up two menus and a water pitcher.

They followed her to a cozy corner. Theirs was the only table with a red rose. The place settings were across from each other, but after Nick seated her, he sat kitty-corner from her and shifted his silverware and napkin in front of him.

She kind of liked how he took charge to sit closer to her.

The hostess handed them the menus and filled their glasses with ice water then left them.

Jasmine opened the menu and scanned down the page, then closed it.

Nick arched a eyebrow. "You've figured out what you want already?"

"Mmm. I was making sure they still had their fabulous filet mignon."

Nick closed his menu. "Sounds good to me."

The server stopped at their table. "I'm Tammy and I'll be your server tonight. You have your choice of three wines—"

"None for me." She grimaced at her too quick response.

Nick squinted at her for a couple of seconds, and shrugged. "None for me either."

Jasmine touched his arm and a tingle ran through her, making her almost wish she hadn't done it. She wouldn't be able to talk to him or eat if she couldn't get her mind off wanting to kiss him. "You don't have to do that for me."

He took her hand, but she drew it away. "No. It's all right. If you're not drinking, I won't either." He gazed up at the server. "We're ready to order, and we'll both have the filet mignon."

"Six- or twelve-ounce, and how do you want it cooked?"

Nick waited for her to state her preference.

"I'll have the six ounce, medium."

He handed both menus to the server. "I'll have the twelve ounce, also medium." He focused on Jasmine. "Do you want to order something to drink or just have water?"

Jasmine glanced at the server. "I'll have mineral water with lemon."

Nick nodded at his glass. "I'll just have the water."

Tammy smiled. "I'll get this put in, and be right back with your drink." She hurried away.

Nick sipped his water. "So, what have you been doing since, um, your uncle took over?"

She leaned toward him and whispered. "You aren't a spy for him, are you?"

His eyes widened, and he shook his head.

She grinned. It had mostly been a joke. If he wanted, her uncle could find someone within the company to spy on her at the office. "I'm still working at Kennedy Holdings in the early learning-the-ropes stage, so I don't think Uncle Dean feels threatened by me. And he's always liked me." She leaned closer and whispered. "I'm the one who's spying. He won't let Josh into the building." Josh being barred had been splashed across the news. No surprise there, but it was unexpectedly comfortable talking to Nick about it.

"I'm so sorry."

"It's all right. We haven't given up. Enough of that. Tell me about your business." Jasmine sucked in a breath and widened her eyes. "No! Forget I asked that. Tell me about where you grew up." She couldn't believe she'd almost gotten him started on the topic that had bored her with last year's auction winner.

"I grew up in Stewartville, Minnesota, just south of Rochester."

She tipped her head. "You make it sound like I should know Rochester."

"It's where one of the Mayo Clinics is."

Jasmine nodded. "Oh, that's big. I think we've made some donations to them. So, brothers, sisters, other family?"

He grinned. "Brother and sister. Mom and Dad still live in the house I grew up in. My sister, Tricia, is single. Well, divorced and no kids. My brother, Rob, is three years younger and lives in Florida."

She faked a shiver. "He couldn't take those Minnesota winters any longer?"

Nick chuckled. "Rob followed his girlfriend, Ruth, down there. They're married now with two kids. Maybe his wife couldn't take the winters."

She slid her hand from her lap to halfway to her stomach, but froze. Dead giveaway. She probably wouldn't see Nick again, so no sense going into that. "So, you're an uncle. Niece, nephew?"

"Both. Emily's four, a cute little thing. And Jackson is a couple months old. I haven't seen him yet."

"I guess you don't see them often." She hadn't figured out if he liked children, but she didn't need to know that. This was a first date. He'd paid a lot of money to spend time with her, and she didn't know why.

"Every three or four months I fly down for long weekends. I used to watch out for my little brother, so I like to check up on him."

She leaned her chin on her hand. "That's nice. My brother is really protective."

A loud laugh burst from him. "Yeah, I noticed, though I'm glad you have someone in your corner."

She loved his laugh and wanted to hear more of it. He finished so seriously, as if he cared for her already. There was some kind of connection with him she'd never had with another guy, and it had developed surprisingly fast.

"Here we go." The server stood over them, two steamy plates in her hands. She set the steaks before them. "Be careful. They're hot."

Throughout dinner, they shared childhood stories. She

hadn't laughed so much in years.

Tammy returned with a tray of luscious desserts. "I hope you've saved room for dessert."

Half of them were chocolate. Her favorite. "I shouldn't."

Tammy rested the tray on the edge of their table. "It's included with your meal, but I could box it up if you'd like to take it home."

"Okay. Then yes."

Nick leaned forward. "We could split one if you want."

That sounded so...intimate. And perfect. As if they'd known each other longer than these couple of hours. "Okay. What do you want?"

"It all looks wonderful to me, so you get to choose."

She studied the tray. Definitely chocolate. Not the smaller desserts, since they would share. She pointed. "How about chocolate cake with a side of vanilla ice cream?"

Tammy smiled. "Seven Layer Decadence. One of my favorites. I'll be back shortly."

Their evening was almost over, and Jasmine didn't want it to end. Her life was so complicated right now, but she wanted to fit Nick into it. "So, tell me about your company." She did not just say that.

"I thought we weren't supposed to talk about it."

She laughed. "I know, but I don't think you'd make it boring and all about you, like my last auction date did."

"Ah." His eyes glowed in a too familiar way. "I started thinking about it when I was in college. Every few months, the school's computers were down because hackers attacked the network. Sometimes they'd be down for a day, sometimes longer. I don't know if information was stolen or if the purpose was to cause problems. I decided they needed better protection. By the time I graduated, I had my anti-hacker software almost ready to go."

She tipped her head and squinted at him. "Kind of like

anti-virus software?"

"Not exactly."

"Wow." He was smart but didn't act as if he was better than others.

"To have real-world testing, I offered it free to my college. In the six years since they've had it, they've only been hacked once. And I fixed it, so it won't happen the same way again."

"That's amazing." The diners all around them had faded into nothing. She couldn't keep her eyes off him, and his voice held soothing qualities that wrapped around her.

He was proud of his accomplishments, and she somehow felt included in them.

The server stopped beside them. "Here you go. Enjoy." She set the plate between them with an even larger piece of cake than the sample, a scoop of ice cream on each side, and a small dish filled with hot fudge sauce. Two forks rested on the plate.

Jasmine lifted the dish and held it over the cake. "Do you mind?"

"Be my guest."

She dumped it evenly over the dark layers and scraped the last out with a spoon then stuck it in her mouth. Warm chocolate was the best.

"You've got fudge on your lip." Before she could dab it with her napkin, Nick rubbed the spot with his thumb, then licked off the chocolate.

Her heart kicked up into the stratosphere. Jasmine had no idea how this man could affect her so deeply. She stared into his eyes as she picked up her fork. Nick turned the plate so the frosting side faced her.

She laughed. She took a bite of cake that was half frosting and closed her eyes. "Hmm. That is so good."

She opened her eyes and found him watching her. His

expression was enough to cause a catch in her breath. Sexy didn't cover it. It excited her and made her too nervous to keep staring at him. His hot expression was more decadent than the cake.

She scooped up another piece. "You have to try this."

Before she could eat it, he grabbed her hand, leaned close and devoured the cake from her fork, all the while staring into her eyes.

He let go of her hand, and she left it poised between them. Heat spiraled down her middle, and she sucked in a breath, pretty sure it had been a while since the last one.

He removed the fork from her nerveless fingers and took her hand. "Come...on another date with me."

She'd enjoyed the evening more than with any other man, and didn't want to never see him again. "I'd like that."

His face lit up. "Friday? My friend's sister is in this off-Broadway play, and he says it's pretty good. We could meet up with them afterward for dessert or something."

"Okay. It sounds fun."

He grinned. "Thank you. Now, let's dig into this cake."

The sexual tension dissolved, and she enjoyed her half of the cake and settle into an easy banter with Nick.

And then it was time to leave. She didn't want the evening to be over, but she was tired. Late nights didn't work for her anymore.

He flagged down a cab, and they got in then she gave her address. Much too soon they turned into the circular drive.

"Wow. This is impressive," Nick said.

She studied the house, trying to see it with his eyes. She'd lived there most of her life and it was just home. "I guess it is big."

"And wonderful architecture." He leaned toward the cab driver. "I'll just be a few minutes."

He swung the door opened, got out and assisted her.

They climbed the four steps side-by-side and stopped in front of the door. She hadn't done this since high school. Usually a date stopped in front of the house, and she ran up the steps alone. Or she took a cab home from wherever they'd met.

He held her hands in his. "I had a wonderful evening. I'm looking forward to Friday. I can pick you up at five, and we'll have an early dinner before the show, or I can pick you up at six-thirty, in time for the show."

"Dinner would be nice."

"Five it is. Goodnight, Jasmine." He kissed her—an all too short kiss, leaving her wanting more. He reached the car and spun around. He kissed his fingers and held them out toward her, as if he was reluctant to leave. "Until Friday."

She touched her lips, half ready to run back down the stairs and fling herself into his arms. But she didn't. It was crazy to be this attracted to him already. After waving, she entered the house, and leaned back against the door. Dinner had been immensely enjoyable. Although she'd been immediately attracted to him the night of the auction, she'd half expected those feelings would be gone upon seeing him again. The evening had ended way too soon. She let out a long sigh.

Josh stepped into the entry. "That bad, huh?"

She hugged him. "No. That good. He wasn't a cardboard guy. We're going to a play on Friday."

A long time ago, she'd started a joke about the cardboard guys she dated. Mostly, they were men who required a date for some function or she needed one for a charity event. She rarely got past one date. All they wanted was an attractive, rich woman on their arm and didn't treat her like a real person, just a means to an end.

Nick hadn't seemed to care who saw them. He'd only had eyes for her. And she couldn't wait to see him again.

Chapter 5

Nick had thought of nothing but Jasmine and their next date since leaving her on her doorstep. He'd nearly slipped and asked her to come home with him. That would have gotten him an emphatic 'no' and likely another 'no' if he backpedaled to ask for this date. The same something that had connected them the one evening and night months ago still simmered inside him.

He paced Alex's apartment and checked his watch a third time. Muted cheers erupted from the television. Usually, Nick would be glued to the screen, cheering with the crowd at whoever made a run, but a date with Jasmine was more important than any game.

He'd asked Alex about attire for the small theater, and had been told that the audience included men in jeans to suits. He wanted to look his best for Jasmine, so chose his black business suit.

Five more minutes and he could leave, arriving a few minutes early at Jasmine's.

Alex shook his head. "You're going to wear a hole in my floor. Sit down."

Nick glared at his friend, and dropped into a chair. His leg bounced. "You know how important this is."

Alex muted the game on TV. "I bet if someone tried to steal Prime Secure from you, you'd be less stressed than you are right now."

Nick ran a hand through his hair. "This has to work out." She'd been on his mind since day one, and the auction date had only made him more interested in her.

Alex laced his fingers behind his head. "Hey, just be yourself. If she doesn't like you that way, then she's not the girl for you."

Nick raised a brow. "And why would I take advice from a guy whose last girlfriend left him?"

Alex clenched a hand to his chest. "Hey, that's a low blow. It took me a while to figure out Sierra wasn't the right woman for me. She figured it out sooner."

Nick stuck a hand in his jacket pocket. "Sorry. I'll calm down when I'm with Jasmine." He checked his watch again. Finally! He jumped up. "Gotta go."

Alex chuckled. "Good luck. I'll see you at the theater."

He could imagine Alex asking Jasmine something about their first evening and turned back. "Don't mention anything about when I first met Jasmine. She doesn't remember it, and it's best left that way for now. Got it?"

Alex saluted. "Got it."

The theater was far enough off Broadway to have parking, so he drove his car. Back home in his small hometown, his atomic-silver Lexus GSF stood out, but in New York, it blended in with the other high-end cars.

Dealing with traffic took his mind off Jasmine. Mostly. He hadn't expected more jitters than when he saw her at the charity event or went out on their auction date. It almost felt like his first date in high school, and wondering if he should kiss the girl at the end. He'd given her a short goodnight kiss on the last date, and he tried not to think about the kinds of steamy kisses they'd shared the first time they'd met.

He stopped in front of the three-story mansion and dragged in a breath. A glance at the clock before turning off the car told him he was only five minutes early. He got out, hurried up the steps and rang the doorbell, listening to its vaguely familiar tune.

The door swung open. He'd hoped Jasmine would answer it. Instead Josh's hostile glare greeted him. Jasmine's brother wore jeans and a t-shirt, and despite the expression, it made Nick more comfortable. Now, he had to get into this man's good graces. If Josh didn't like him, he'd have a harder time getting Jasmine to trust him.

Nick held out his hand. "Good to see you again, Josh."

Josh shook with him. "I'll reserve judgment. She's not ready yet, so come on in."

Nick tried not to gawk like an oaf. He had money now, but this was old money. The pecan-colored hardwood he stepped across gleamed. Wide baseboards, crown molding, and graceful stairs echoed the hue. Those stairs would be perfect for Jasmine to come down in a wedding dress with her skirt trailing behind her. He shook his head. Much too soon for thoughts like that.

He picked up his pace, and followed Josh into a living room, a grand and formal room that he didn't expect to look lived in. A big screen TV hung across from a tan, suede leather couch. Matching loveseats at each end sat at right angles. Farther down the room, two groupings of four chairs provided a space for private conversations. Two wide windows with window seats let in light. A paperback rested in the center of the left one. He'd bet it was Jasmine's favorite reading spot, and itched to see what book she was reading.

"Done with your inspection?" Josh said with distain.

Yeah. A lot of work needed with Josh.

"I'm curious about the place Jasmine calls home. This looks like a comfortable room."

Josh's shoulders dropped a bit. "This *is* her favorite

room. Look, I'm trying to protect Jasmine. She doesn't need someone who's after her money."

"I'm glad she has you in her corner. My sole interest is Jasmine. She's beautiful and smart. I'm sure you had me checked out, and know I don't need anyone's money. And I don't intend on hurting her."

"Ah…guys."

They both turned. Jasmine stood inside the doorway, and she took his breath away, as always. The top of her red dress hugged her breasts, and revealed a hint of cleavage. A gathered skirt flared a bit and ended at her knees. Small heels on her black shoes lifted her enough to define her calves, and the strap emphasized her delicate ankles.

Nick crossed the room in seconds. "Hi, beautiful." It took everything in him not to kiss her in front of her brother. As far as she remembered, he'd only kissed her once, and he recalled all of them.

She smiled. "Hi, Nick. Sorry about the overbearing brother."

He focused on Josh. "It's all right. He cares about you. I respect that." He gazed at her, wanting to remove all the pins from her hair and run his hands through it like he'd done that first night. "You ready?"

"Yes. Bye, Josh."

Nick escorted her out the door and into his car, then got into the driver's seat. "I chose a restaurant near the theater. I haven't been there, so I don't know how the food is."

"Oh, what's it called?"

"Matthew's Place."

She gasped, smiling.

He grinned, enjoying pleasing her. "You've been there?"

She tapped her feet on the floor. "No, but I've heard they have great food, and I've wanted to go."

"Good. We get to try it together."

The GPS guided him to the restaurant, and he pulled into the lane for valet parking. The uniformed man helped Jasmine out of the vehicle and handed Nick the ticket.

Nick led Jasmine inside, and up to the reservation desk. The crisply dressed redhead finished typing on a screen and glanced up at him.

"I have a reservation. Lawson."

"Ah. Mr. Lawson." The woman picked up two menus from the stack behind her. "This way, please."

Nick followed behind the hostess and Jasmine. The tables were occupied by well dressed men and women talking in subdued voices. The hostess stopped at a small booth in the corner. Good. As private as they could get in a restaurant.

"Wayne will be taking care of you tonight."

A wine menu rested in the center of the table, and Nick picked it up. He preferred something else, but would stick with wine tonight. "What would you like to drink?"

"Iced tea, please."

"Are you sure? They've got some outstanding wines on the list."

"I'm sure."

She'd probably been afraid to drink since the night of her father's funeral. He couldn't imagine what had gone through her head when she woke up in a stranger's room. He wished he'd had a chance to talk to her before she left, ease her mind about what had happened between them. And get her full name and number. If he hadn't seen her on the news report, he might never have found her.

Now, he had a chance to do it right.

A man with a small leather folder approached. "I'm Wayne. I'll be your server. Would you like to start with a drink?"

Nick nodded toward Jasmine. "She'll have ice tea. Sweet or unsweet?"

"Sweet, please."

"I'll have a glass of your house red." He didn't know wines, and preferred a beer, but the atmosphere seemed to prohibit it.

After the server left, they discussed the menu and made their selections.

Wayne swooped in. "Here you go. Tea and wine." He set glasses before them. "Now what can I get you?"

Wayne took their order and left. Nick sipped from his glass. "Do you ever drink alcohol?"

Her gaze darted up to him and then to her tea. He detected a hint of a blush. "I'm taking a break for a while."

He squeezed her hand. Her reaction was another thing that told him getting drunk was unusual for her. "Hey, I'm not pushing. I was just curious. Does it bother you if I drink?"

"Not at all." She grinned. "I can be the designated driver."

He chuckled. "I'm only having one glass. So tell me, what do you like to do when you're not working?"

"I like to take walks."

"In Minnesota, I'm used to hiking. Where do you walk?" Maybe he could take her out of the city for a walk in the woods.

"Mostly around the neighborhood. And there's a park a couple of blocks away."

"What else do you do?"

"I get together with friends. We'll go out to eat or have a girls' night." She wrinkled her nose. "Or go shopping."

He grinned. "You don't like shopping?" He couldn't imagine a woman with no budget who didn't like shopping.

She shrugged. "Sometimes. If I need something specific. But Anna loves shopping, and she'll coerce me into going. I'll buy quality. I mean, I have to dress well for work since

I'm part owner. It's amazing though what Anna will find on clearance and discount racks."

Nick could imagine Jasmine good-naturedly following her friend from rack to rack. "For the most part, I don't care what I wear, but for my business, I have to look the part of a successful business owner. I sweat bullets when I had to get fitted for my first expensive suit."

She touched his hand, sending a spark up his arm, and laughed. He loved the sound of it. Her eyes glittered. "I remember when I got my first formal dress. Mom and I both picked out dresses, and mine had to be altered. It was so embarrassing standing half naked while I got measured."

He remembered when she stood half naked in front of him, not at all embarrassed. Ready for what came next, but, as he knew now, not knowing what that was. She'd been gorgeous, the sexiest woman he'd ever seen.

Nick cleared his throat. "How about sports?"

"I played tennis in college. Not on a team, just meet-ups at the courts. I joined the swim team, but I hated all the practice. It made me not enjoy swimming, so I quit."

"I played basketball in high school, but didn't do sports in college. I concentrated on my academics. I still exercise, just nothing organized. Do you still volunteer reading at that public school?"

She frowned. Her response was slow. "Yees. Once a month."

He realized his error. She'd told him about volunteering when they first met. There was no way he should know about it. He'd only make it worse by coming up with a reason for knowing. "I'd like to do something like that once I get settled into my new office."

She eagerly talked about her experiences and the children, hopefully forgetting his slip-up.

Conversation with Jasmine introduced new insights. She

had varied interests and strong opinions on some topics, and he enjoyed the playful debate. The more time he spent with her, the more he needed to have her in his life.

~~~

It was a nice old theater. Jasmine could imagine how it had glowed in its early days with shiny chrome and bright lights. The name of the play was displayed in big black letters on the marquee. *Agatha Christie's The Unexpected Guest.*

She grabbed his arm and immediately released it. "Oh, I love Agatha Christie."

He smiled. "I hope her plays are as good as her books."

"Have you read *Murder on the Orient Express*, or seen any of the movies?"

"No. I haven't read that book, and I missed the movies."

"I loved its twists. I'm sure this will be great." He hadn't told her what play they'd see, and she'd thought the worst. It would be some boring, highbrow nonsense he thought *she* might like. Maybe he knew her after all.

Nick presented his tickets, and they were shown to their seats, fourth row, near the middle.

His friend jumped up, and held out his hand. "So, this is the lovely Jasmine. I'm Alex."

"Hi, Alex. It's nice meeting you. Nick's had nice things to say about you."

"Of course he has. I'm a nice guy. You're going to love Beth's performance. This is her first lead, and she's terrific." He glanced around. "We better sit."

Alex nudged Nick into the seats first which placed her between the two men. She had a feeling that wasn't the seating order Nick had intended.

The curtain rose, and she became engrossed in the show.

She hated the rolling emotions since she'd gotten

pregnant. Jasmine fished a tissue from her purse and tried to wipe her eyes without Nick noticing. He lifted a brow and took her hand. Who cried when the woman in the play looked guilty as sin and at how her husband had mistreated her? She did, apparently.

He leaned in. "Are you okay?"

"I'm fine. It's…Beth's a good actress."

It took a while for her to return her attention to the play after Nick draped his arm along her shoulders and kissed her temple. She hoped he wouldn't wonder about the reason for her emotional shifts.

The play ended and Jasmine clapped enthusiastically. The three chatted about the various off-Broadway theaters in the area for the fifteen minutes before Beth joined them.

Jasmine and Nick walked hand-in-hand behind the siblings to a café a couple of blocks away. She'd been startled when he captured her hand and nearly pulled it away. A quick glance found him watching her. He lifted their joined hands and kissed the back of hers.

Her breath caught, and she had to look away. She wasn't getting enough oxygen with her quick shallow breaths and sucked in a long one. She'd always thought those Victorian novels where the heroine got fluttery over having her hand kissed were ridiculous. Now, she'd read them with a whole new sense of understanding.

The restaurant was a seat-yourself place, and Beth led the way to a booth. The women sat across from each other next to the wall. They ordered desserts, but this time she and Nick weren't sharing.

His shoulder brushed hers occasionally when he moved, sending warmth tingling up her arm and into her chest. Then he shifted, and his leg touched hers—and he left it there. Her hand shook a bit when she sipped her lemon water. No man had ever had the effect on her that Nick did with just a touch.

45

Conversation swirled around her, and she had to concentrate.

"I'm already reading the next script," Beth said.

Jasmine ran a finger up and down the condensation on her glass. "Are you the lead again?"

Beth shook her head. "The lead is a man, but I've got the best female part."

Jasmine momentarily clasped the woman's hand. "You deserve it. You were wonderful."

"Thanks."

Alex grinned and wrapped an arm around his sister. "This kid has been stealing the show since her first performance in kindergarten."

Beth bumped her brother with her shoulder, and he released her. "I've always loved acting. I fell in love with it more when Mom took us to some of these off-Broadway plays."

"Speak for yourself, kid."

Beth smiled. "Yeah, after a couple, Alex begged off." She leaned forward. "The performers in a play are more real than what you see on TV or the movie screen. It was almost like I could touch them. I told myself, I can do that." She spread her hands. "So, here I am."

The waitress approached. "And here you are." She winked at Beth, and set a delicious looking dessert in front of each of them.

Jasmine dug into her brownie sundae. "Mmm." They'd warmed the homemade brownie, and the sprinkle of walnuts on top of the whipped cream made it perfect.

Nick had chosen apple pie, which she liked, but it didn't look half as good as her dessert. He held his second bite turned toward her. "Want to try it?"

She almost told him no, but got caught up in the glow in his eyes. She leaned closer, opening her mouth, and he brought the forkful to her lips. It was a bigger mouthful than she'd usually take. Their eyes locked as she chewed and swallowed. "It's good, but doesn't beat my brownie."

He wiggled his fingers in a come on gesture. "Prove it."

She knew he wanted her to feed him a bite the way he had her. She cut a piece of brownie and scooped it up with fudge and ice cream, holding it out to him. Like last time, his hand enclosed hers as he devoured the treat.

"Aw. That's so sweet," Beth said.

She'd totally forgotten about their audience, and her face heated. She ducked her head and prepared another bite for herself.

Conversation slowed to a trickle as they ate.

The waitress brought the check, and Nick snatched it up. "Hold on." He fished out his wallet and handed over his credit card.

"I can pay half," Alex said.

Nick waggled his wallet. "I didn't have to pay for the play, so this is on me. Besides, I owe you more than that for putting up with me at your place."

"You'd do the same for me."

The waitress returned, and Nick added a tip and signed the slip. "It's been a nice evening. Thank you, Beth, for the tickets. I'm taking Jasmine home now." He stood.

Jasmine squeezed Beth's hand. "It was so nice meeting you. I really enjoyed your performance." She took Alex's hand. "It was nice meeting you, too, Alex."

The others slid out of their seats when she did.

Beth gave her a hug. "I hope we'll see each other again."

Jasmine pulled her phone from her purse. "Let's plan on it." They exchanged numbers, then they walked back to the parking lot beside the theater. Jasmine waved to the others as Nick opened her door.

She leaned back, closed her eyes, and blew out a breath.

It had been an enjoyable evening, but long. Nick got in beside her and started the car.

His lips touched hers and she jumped, her eyes flying open.

He grinned. "Sorry. I couldn't resist."

Sitting beside him for hours had made her crave him, and that short kiss wasn't enough. She placed a hand on his shoulder and leaned into him. Twisting in the car was a bit awkward, but she didn't want to wait until she got home to kiss him.

He took over the kiss and made her hungry for more. His hand slipped from her back to her breast. She squeezed his shoulder and moaned, almost not believing that sound came from her.

A tap-tap on the window startled her and she leaned back against the seat, closing her eyes. Everything besides Nick had fled her mind as they kissed. It would have come to a screeching halt if his hand had drifted lower to her stomach.

Nick rolled down the window.

"Sorry, sir," a masculine voice said. "You're the last car in the lot and I need to chain it closed for the night."

Nick leaned forward a little—maybe to better hide her. "Sorry. We'll leave now."

He put the car in gear and rolled up the window. "Sorry, Jasmine. I haven't been caught necking in my car since I was a teenager."

She straightened in her seat. "It was a first for me. Not something I ever aspired to."

He pulled onto the street and grinned. "But it was worth it."

She was glad it was dark enough he couldn't see her face flame. It *was* worth it, but she'd never admit to it.

In the lighter traffic, they reached Jasmine's home in half the time as the earlier drive. With a hand at her back, Nick walked her to the door. "That in the car was not a goodnight kiss."

"Why not?" She was glad he wasn't done kissing her, but some dates had given her a quick peck on the cheek and sent her home or to her door. Of course, she'd encouraged that response.

Nick took her face between his hands. "Because it only made me want to kiss you more." Oh, those lips of his, they might be warmer than before. Maybe he'd anticipated this as much as she had. She loved the tongue duel they did. It made her want more, and she started to sway toward him, but at the last moment remembered he'd feel the small swell of her belly. She didn't want that explanation right now.

He pulled back slowly and stared into her eyes. "Goodnight, my Jasmine."

"Goodnight, Nick."

"I'll call you."

If she didn't have her brother waiting inside, and didn't have to explain her pregnancy, she would have invited him in. Or maybe the roadblocks made her feel bold because she knew she couldn't do it.

Chapter 6

Two weeks later, Nick had moved into his apartment. It was nice to have his own space again. The next day, as previously planned, he and Alex got together to watch a baseball game. Nick brought the food and Alex provided the drink.

Alex clicked the remote and turned on the game. "I found out something today I don't think you're going to like."

Nick frowned and dropped his slice of pizza back on his plate. "What is it?"

Alex set his plate on his lap and narrowed his eyes. "I was showing a client an apartment, and he told me he wished he had the money to buy a portion of a company that had gone up for sale. It's Kennedy Holdings."

"What? The evil uncle is selling the company?" It would kill Jasmine. It was hard enough to lose control, but now it would be totally gone.

"Not the whole company. Ten percent."

"Ten percent? Did he say how much they wanted for it?"

"He didn't say. What? You want to buy it?"

Nick rubbed the back of his neck. He'd do anything to keep her happy. "If I can swing it, I'm buying it for Jasmine."

Alex snickered. "That's some wedding present."

Nick glared. He'd seen Jasmine several times in the past

couple of weeks, and each time he fell a little more in love with her. She had a subtle humor that crept up on him, and she didn't just care about others, she did something to help them.

Alex lifted his hands and grinned. "What? It's got to be serious if you'd spend millions for her."

Wanting to buy those shares was a knee jerk reaction to protect Jasmine, but he had to try. Alex was right. Giving Jasmine back the portion of her company she thought had been lost would be a spectacular wedding present. "Yes, I love her, and I'm calling my lawyer first thing tomorrow."

~~~

Jasmine turned sideways in front of the mirror. With the jeans button undone, and the loose fitting t-shirt, she didn't think she appeared pregnant. She rubbed the small bump. At four months, she wouldn't be able to hide it much longer. But she should get through another day.

One more day to fall even more in love with Nick. She didn't know how it had happened. Her life was a disaster, but Nick was the best part of it. Her only fear about the baby was possibly losing Nick when she told him. The worst part would be telling him she didn't know who the baby's father was. Even she had found it hard to believe, with the baby evidence, that she'd had sex only one night in her life, and didn't remember most of it.

She found it hard to believe she'd had sex at all, only remembering bits and pieces. Kisses. Heavy breathing. His lips on her neck and shoulders. The excitement. Thinking about it made her feel like there was more. Obviously, there was more. That's what she wanted, and Nick was the one she wanted it with. But when he found out, would he think she wasn't who he thought she was?

Jasmine sighed and forced the thoughts away. She'd find out his reaction soon enough.

Now for breakfast before he arrived. Eggs were off the menu, but otherwise, her nausea was gone. There was only a small amount of food on the table since Josh was away. She ate two strips of bacon and a bowl of oatmeal then took her dishes to the kitchen, and put them in the dishwasher.

Lydia shook her head, and wrapped an arm around Jasmine's shoulders. "When your wee one gets bigger, I'm going to force you to let me come collect the dishes."

Jasmine hugged her. "That'll only happen if I'm put on bed rest. You never told Mom not to bring the dishes into the kitchen."

Lydia chuckled. "That's because I gave up."

Jasmine's mother hadn't come from money, and had instilled in Josh and Jasmine that the household staff were not to be treated as slaves like she'd seen in other wealthy homes.

Jasmine patted her tummy. "Well, for now, you lost with me, too." She exited the kitchen.

With a half-hour remaining before Nick arrived, she could settle with a book. After seeing the Agatha Christie play with Nick a couple weeks ago, she'd started a kick of her favorite Miss Marple mysteries from her home library. She curled up on the couch to start the fifth one.

The chimes of the doorbell woke her. Her book had slipped to the couch cushion, and her head rested on the arm. She dropped the book on the side table, stood, stretched and rubbed her eyes.

She opened the door as the bell pealed again. Nick caused her heart to leap.

He smiled and touched her cheek. "You look like you just woke up. You have a crease here."

She touched the spot, and a blush crept up from her neck. "I fell asleep reading. I'm fine." She opened the door wider.

"Do you want to come in and sit down, or are we leaving right away?"

"We'll go, if you're sure you're all right."

She kissed his cheek. "You're so thoughtful, but I'm fine. Let me get my shoes." As she put them on, she studied him. He looked good in jeans and his tucked in t-shirt. He must work out. He didn't have huge muscles, but big enough to be strong. And those dark, chocolate eyes made her heart flutter every time he looked at her. She picked up her purse from the table. "I'm ready."

"You might want to grab a jacket. It's going to be cool."

He hadn't told her what they were doing. She selected a light-weight windbreaker from the closet. "This one?"

"That'll do."

They got in the waiting cab, and wove through traffic. A half-hour later, they pulled into Battery Park and the cab stopped in front of the ferry port.

"The Statue of Liberty." She stared at the monument in the harbor.

Nick paid the driver and helped her out of the cab.

"The last time I was here, I was thirteen." She turned from Nick as she wiped tears from her cheeks.

He stepped in front of her and clutched her arms. "Jasmine, what's wrong?" Leave it to Nick to be so attentive. The concern in his eyes almost caused fresh tears, but she fought them back.

"Mom brought Josh and me here. That day is so clear in my mind." No, she couldn't keep the tears stemmed. "It was the last outing she took us on before she died."

Nick wrapped his arms around her. "Honey, I'm so sorry. I had no idea. I wouldn't do anything to intentionally cause you pain."

His warm protection seeped into her. Sure, she got hugs from Josh, but they were nothing like this. Disappointment hit when he pulled back.

"Do you want to leave?"

She touched his cheek. "No. It just caught me by surprise. We had a great day together. It was a good memory. I want to do this with you." She gave him the best smile she could.

He took her hand, and they followed signs to the gate. "I have tickets already, and hopefully the line is short."

Somehow, Nick got them through ticketing and security with a minimum of effort. He held her hand as they boarded the ferry. "Inside or outside?"

She grinned. "Outside. At the top."

The first flight of stairs was crowded, and they had to pause as they worked their way up. Jasmine enjoyed Nick's hand on her back, reassurance he was close. More than half the crowd got off on the second floor, so the next flight moved faster.

They stepped onto the upper deck and Nick grabbed her hand and tugged. "Let's go to the front."

She giggled, and hurried to keep pace. He found an opening at the rail for them, not quite in the bow and wrapped an arm around her waist. "Do you want to sit, or is this all right?"

"This is good. It's a short ride. And if I get cold, you can keep me warm." She turned her head away, surprised at the words that popped out of her mouth.

He chuckled. "I can do that." He stepped behind her and wrapped his arms around her, whispering in her ear. "Might as well preempt the cold."

This was perfect. She covered his arms with hers, grateful he'd kept them above her baby bump. She leaned back into him and he snuggled her closer, kissing her temple.

All too soon, the ferry slid into its slip at the dock. They were almost the last to exit, and worked their way into the building, following signs for the entrance to the statue's crown. As they climbed the stairs, Jasmine was glad an older couple was in front of them. They stopped twice, each time the woman apologized for holding them up, and Jasmine silently thanked them as she caught her breath.

Jasmine hadn't climbed to the crown with her mother and Josh. It was nice to recall the memories of that day and have a unique visit with Nick.

She enjoyed seeing the structure more than the view from the top. Nick wrapped his arms around her as they viewed the New York skyline. She could have stayed there for hours, safe in his arms. She twisted her head around, and when he tipped his head down, she kissed him. He turned her so she almost faced him and deepened the kiss. The longing for more made her dizzy, and she hoped there would be many more times like this. Even after she told him about the baby. She couldn't keep it a secret much longer. She had to tell him soon, but not today. Josh had warned her it would be better for her to tell Nick than for him to finally notice her growing abdomen. She was too afraid of losing him.

~~~

Nick loosened his tie and leaned back in the comfortable chair in front of his lawyer's desk. To the side, he had a great view of Central Park and tall buildings beyond it. Of course, Cyrus Vetros had as good a view straight in front of him in his corner office.

"Give me an update." Nick tried his hardest to indicate this wasn't as important to him as it was. Even in front of his own lawyer, he didn't want to show how the purchase affected him. It had been four weeks since he'd found out about the sale. He'd poured over financial statements and felt comfortable with his decision, but everything was still up in the air.

"The other bidders have dropped out." He pressed his lips together.

Nick smiled. "Is there a problem?"

"He wants more money."

Nick straightened. "That's ridiculous. He's lost all his leverage. Why should I pay more?"

Cyrus dropped his stack of papers on the desk. "He thinks you want it bad enough that you'll pay up."

"I'd be just as happy if there were no buyers, and the company stays in one piece." Damn. He shouldn't have said that. As someone interested in the purchase, his only concern would be buying that piece of the company, not having any hope it might not sell at all. "Don't tell him that. If he wants to sell, his only choice is me, at my last offer."

Cyrus nodded once. "I'll let him know."

"How's my financing coming?"

"We've cashed in the shares you specified, closed out accounts and accumulated it all into one account. The bank is ready for you to sign papers whenever you are. And the paperwork is complete for your new company, Prime Properties."

"Good." He hadn't expected it to cost as much as it had. He'd pulled together fifteen million and put up half of Prime Secure as collateral for the other fifteen million. With the past record of Kennedy Holdings, he'd net a profit even after his loan payment.

Never before in his life would he have jeopardized his company for a woman, but here he was doing it, without a qualm. In a short time, Jasmine had come to mean so much to him that he couldn't imagine life without her.

"And the contract states I get to place a person of my choosing on the board of directors?" Maybe with his proxy on the board he could make changes for Jasmine and Josh.

"Yes. I don't see how he would have a problem with that."

"Let's hope not, because it all falls apart if he objects."

Nick couldn't tell Jasmine until after the sale was complete. He feared that if Dean Kennedy got wind of Nick's association with Jasmine, the sale would collapse. It might be best to wait until his proxy had a secure footing on the board.

Chapter 7

Nick rang the doorbell at the mansion. He and Jasmine had gone out the last two Wednesday evenings, and spent most of the day together for the last two Saturdays. The more time he spent with her, the more he needed to be with her.

This Saturday morning, he planned on taking her to Central Park for a carriage ride. He'd stopped by a deli and had put together a picnic lunch.

He'd decided when they stopped for lunch, he would tell her they'd met in January. He knew her well enough he thought she'd accept it without a problem. She wouldn't likely otherwise find out, but it was the right thing to do. There was that small fear it would blow up in his face. If that happened, he'd work harder to get her to understand how much he cared for her.

Jasmine opened the door. He smiled, then noticed dark smudges under her eyes. He sobered, leaning in closer and touched her cheek. "Honey, you look like you didn't get much sleep. Are you sick?"

She grabbed his hand and dragged him inside. "Oh, Nick. I shouldn't let it bother me this much, but yesterday I found out Uncle Dean is selling ten percent of Kennedy Holdings. He could have sold one of the companies we control, but he's selling part of us. Dad would never have done this."

"So, he announced it to the company?"

"No. I overheard two board members arguing."

He rubbed a hand up and down her back.

"It wasn't like this when Dad was alive."

"Do you know why he's selling?" Nick's attorney hadn't known, which wasn't a surprise.

"No. There are reserves if he wanted to buy into another company. I just don't understand it."

It broke his heart to see how upset she was over the loss of a portion of her father's company. He knew she'd be upset, but it was worse than he expected. He almost told her what he'd done, but the deal wasn't finalized yet, and he could still lose it to an unexpected party. Dean Kennedy wasn't a fair player.

Tears slipped down her cheeks, and she brushed them away. "Sorry. It's the…"

Nick frowned. "It's the what?"

Josh entered the foyer and chuckled. Jasmine glared at him and shook her head vehemently. She seemed to be telling Josh not to say something.

Josh smirked. "The pregnancy hormones."

"Josh!"

Nick's eyes widened, and his attention returned to Jasmine. And her stomach. He'd used a condom, but they weren't a hundred-percent effective. Now that he knew, he wasn't sure how he'd missed it. If he'd held her tightly in his arms, he'd have discovered her condition. He'd wanted to take his time courting her. Do it right this time. He gaze roamed over the loose fitting shirt covering her gently rounded belly, which had been totally flat when they'd made love all those months ago.

He did a quick calculation. "You're five months?"

She gasped. "You can't know that! You're not a doctor."

Yes! One thing he'd learned in the last six weeks,

Jasmine's night with him was out of character. Only one man could be this baby's father. Now, more than ever, he had to make Jasmine believe they belonged together. And it was time to ease her mind on the identity of the baby's father.

She bowed her head. "I was afraid to tell you because I don't want to lose you."

He took her hands in his, ignoring her brother's rapt attention. "You aren't losing me. Even if this baby wasn't mine."

Her head snapped up.

He smiled. "On January twenty-fourth, we had an evening I couldn't forget. I thought I'd never see you again."

Tears glistened in her eyes. "What? It was you? But—" She cupped his cheek. "At first, there were familiar things about you, but the more time I spent with you, it just blended together into you."

"Well, that was unexpected," Josh said. "I should slug you, but you *did* track Jasmine down."

She didn't take her eyes off Nick. "Go away, Josh."

"Hey, I helped make this happen."

Nick winked at her. He'd forgotten Josh was there. Nick would have found out anyway after he told Jasmine they'd been together, but he didn't care how it came out. "Yeah, go away, Josh."

"Fine." He disappeared into the living room.

He kissed her hand. "I saw the news report on the day you lost your father's company. I know that was one of the worst days of your life, but for me, it was the second best day. I found out who you were, so I had a chance of finding you."

Tears slipped down her cheeks. "You wanted to find me?"

Nick wiped away a tear with his thumb. "I wanted to find you more than anything. Remember at the ball when

60

Josh asked why I moved my company to New York?"

She nodded.

"The second answer was the real one. I thought my chances of finding you were better in the city where we met."

Her mouth dropped open. "But it's New York, the biggest city in the country."

"I found you because we were meant to be together." He crushed her to him and kissed her sweet lips. He'd not only found Jasmine, but a family. If he'd hugged her like this before, he might have noticed she was pregnant, but it was important for her to be comfortable with him. She was more than halfway through the pregnancy already, and no matter what, he would be there for the rest and beyond.

She bit her lip. "I'm sorry."

His gut twisted. That wasn't what he expected to hear. Maybe she was getting rid of him now she knew who he was. The words strained his throat. "Sorry about what?"

She touched his face. "That I don't remember you. I remember bits and pieces, but not your face." She blushed, and he wondered what she did remember.

He whispered a sigh of relief. She wanted him. "I'm sorry, too, that I took advantage of you. I thought you were a little tipsy, but I didn't realize you were so intoxicated you wouldn't remember us. And I'm sorry you don't remember your first time."

She wrapped her arms around his neck. "Maybe we can do it again, and I'll recall some memories."

He smiled and kissed her, slipping a hand under the back of her shirt. He'd wanted to touch her from the moment he laid eyes on her again. Her skin was as soft as he remembered. The tight rein he'd put on his desire for her started to slip. "I'm all for making new ones—when the time's right."

She buried her face in his chest. "I've wanted you so

much, but I was afraid of how you'd react to the baby."

He tipped her chin up and chuckled. "Honey, I want you more than ever. When I found out you didn't remember me, it gave me a chance to do it right this time." He tapped her temple. "In here, you're still a virgin, so I didn't want to rush you."

He lifted her and spun around once before lowering her feet to the floor. He slipped a hand between them, and rubbed her stomach. "Wow. We're having a baby."

"So, you're not mad about it?"

"I'm so far from mad, it's in another country." He leaned back. "Are you sure you're up to going out today?"

She tapped his arm. "I'm not an invalid."

He grinned and took her hand. "Okay. Let's go."

This morning, Nick hated New York traffic, and as he maneuvered through it, wished he'd opted for a cab. A twenty-minute ride got them to the parking garage he'd selected. If they'd taken a cab, he could have had it drop them at an entrance. Now Jasmine would have to walk before getting to the park. He found an empty spot in the parking garage and grabbed the soft-sided cooler from the backseat.

"Do you want me to call a cab?"

"We're two blocks from Central Park. I climbed the Statue of Liberty two weeks ago. I can do this." Her voice showed some irritation.

He grinned. Probably a silly grin, but he was extremely happy. "This is new to me. Give me a chance."

Jasmine looped her arm through his. The day was perfect, and they hadn't gotten to the good part yet. *What was he thinking?* Nothing could top finding out about their baby.

Jasmine pointed out squirrels chasing each other and named some of the flowers. He took a left, and a little ways up, the horses and carriages stood in a row. He headed for the park bench nearest them, and set down the cooler. "Have a seat while I find our driver."

Jasmine sat, a gleam in her eye.

Nick headed to the first coachman, and showed his receipt. "Are you Charles?"

The man shook his head. "He's the last man in line."

"Okay, thanks." Nick had prepaid for three hours and had a fifty folded in his pocket for a tip. "Charles?"

The man tipped his hat back. "Yes."

Nick unfolded his paper. "I'm Nick Lawson. I reserved three hours."

"That's longer than we usually go."

"I planned a picnic for the middle of our ride, if you can pick out a good picnic spot. I packed a lunch for you, too. Then we'll finish up the time."

The man nodded, and patted his horse. "Why don't you and your lady get in the carriage while I grab extra water for the horse?"

Nick returned to Jasmine, picked up the cooler and took her hand. "Ready?"

She grinned. "I haven't had a carriage ride since I was—I don't know—eight or nine."

"I hope it's as good as you remember." He slid the cooler under the seat and helped Jasmine into the carriage. She sat and he took the place beside her. Within a few minutes the coachman climbed into his seat and clicked to his horse. They started out with a lurch, and Jasmine giggled.

Nick wrapped his arm around her, drawing her closer. She seemed more relaxed now that he knew she was pregnant. He covered her small belly with his hand and she smiled at him. "A baby. That'll take some getting used to." He couldn't resist giving her a quick kiss.

He enjoyed Jasmine's excitement. They'd been in the carriage an hour already, and she still swung her head from side to side so she wouldn't miss anything. Children pointed, and she waved to them as if she was in a parade.

She gripped his hand and pointed. "Look. It's a rabbit." She pointed in a different direction. "And there's a chipmunk."

He laughed. He'd grown up in Minnesota. Rabbits, chipmunks, and squirrels were a daily sighting. They'd probably been eradicated from her neighborhood, so this was a rare treat.

About an hour-and-half into the drive they skirted the reservoir. Charles stopped the carriage near picnic tables. "How's this?"

Nick nodded. "Perfect. Thank you."

The coachman jumped from the carriage, and set out the step to help them down. Nick slid the cooler next to the side and zipped it open. He glanced at Charles. "Do you want a roast beef or turkey sandwich?"

The man waved his hand. "You don't have to do that."

Nick tipped the bag. "I brought lots of food."

"All right, thanks. I'll take roast beef."

Nick handed it to him, as well as a bag of chips and bottle of water. He took Jasmine's hand. "Picnic table or blanket?"

She laughed. "You must have been a boy scout. Let's use the blanket. We can sit closer to the water."

She helped him spread it in a sunny spot. He removed three sandwiches, chips, her favorite mineral water with a small container of lemon wedges and napkins from the bag. "You're pregnant. That's why you didn't drink. I thought it might have been because you'd gotten intoxicated and forgot our night together. I can't imagine how you felt when you woke up in a stranger's room. Do you remember that part?"

She twisted her hands, staring at them. "Yes. I heard you in the bathroom and panicked."

He covered her hands to still them. "I panicked, too,

when I saw you were gone. I wished I'd taken a faster shower." He grinned. "I've got a souvenir pair of pink panties, if you ever want to try them on like Cinderella."

Her eyes widened, her mouth dropped open, and she blushed.

He squeezed her hands. It wasn't like she was experienced. Just because she knew he was *that* man now didn't mean he shouldn't still treat her with respect. "I'm sorry. I shouldn't have said that."

"It's all right." She stared at their hands. "It's kind of sexy that you still have them."

He chuckled. "Let's eat."

Chapter 8

Nick couldn't believe how excited he was that Jasmine was going to show him off at work. She hadn't actually said that, but she planned to introduce him as her boyfriend to her co-workers. Due to her increasing size, she'd started wearing maternity clothes, so those who hadn't been told she was pregnant would know very soon. And he didn't mind at all if they speculated that the new boyfriend was the father.

He strode through the doors at Kennedy Holdings at eleven-thirty, enough time to meet a few people and make their lunch reservation for noon.

He smiled at the woman sitting at the reception desk. "I'm Nick Lawson, here to see Jasmine Kennedy."

She returned the smile. "Jasmine stopped this morning and said her boyfriend would be coming in today."

"Yes. Expect to see a lot of me."

She held out a card with a clip on it. "Here's your badge. Be sure to return it when you leave." She typed on her screen. "The elevator's down there. Second floor. Take a left. Her office is about halfway down on the right, and her nameplate is beside the door."

He clipped on the badge and got on the elevator and off on the second floor. He stepped out and paused, not remembering if it was right then left, or left then right. He took a right, checking the name plates as he proceeded.

He neared the end when heated, low voices caught his attention. He shouldn't listen, but something bothered him about the angry discussion. The nameplate beside the cracked open door read *Rhonda Whitaker*. He stood against the wall, and pulled out his phone, setting it on silent in case it rang. He started typing a nonsensical text message as an excuse for standing there. Not great, but better than nothing.

"You didn't tell me you were going to sell off part of Kennedy Holdings," the outraged woman said.

"It's my company to do with as I want. There's no reason for me to tell you." Evidently, that was Dean Kennedy.

"I helped make you the chairman because you had more experience than Josh. Now I see I made a mistake. I can sway votes to kick you out, too."

Something rattled, and the woman gasped.

"Listen, bitch. I've got evidence that you got rid of Art because he spurned your advances. Now, you do what I tell you, or you go to prison."

"What!" One loud word before she lowered her voice again. "I thought he had a heart attack." She'd sounded as surprised as Nick felt. "How can you have proof of something I didn't do?"

That was Nick's cue to leave before he got caught. He hurried toward the elevator, stopping when he reached it. Jasmine had been devastated by her father's death, and it turned out, he'd been murdered because of greed.

He rubbed his forehead and ran his fingers through his hair. Jasmine couldn't know yet. The knowledge could put her in danger, or adversely affect the pregnancy. He'd have to talk to Josh after lunch. A couple deep breaths, and he was as ready as he'd ever be to see Jasmine after that shattering news. At her door, he knocked on the jamb.

She tipped her head up, grinned and raced to him. He

laughed as he folded his arms around her. Once she no longer feared his reaction about the baby, she'd spent a lot of time in his arms. As they stood in the doorway, he kissed her, not caring who might see.

She stepped back. "Let me introduce you to some people."

And the world crashed back to normal.

Jasmine led him to the office beside hers. "Hey, Anna, I want you to meet my boyfriend, Nick Lawson. Anna Greenfield."

Anna's thick, blonde hair was cut into a short bob. Her deep blue eyes sparkled. She rounded her desk, and held out her hand. Nick took it and received a firm shake.

"Anna's my best friend."

Jasmine's friend crossed her arms. "I was quite surprised when Jasmine told me her auction boyfriend was the jerk who got her pregnant while she was impaired." Her gaze darted between him and Jasmine. "By the way, she never called you a jerk."

Nick wrapped an arm around Jasmine's waist. "I'm not always a jerk. It's nice she has a supportive friend."

Jasmine hugged Anna. "We've got a couple more people to see before lunch."

They entered the office across the hall. A man perched on the corner of the desk of a pretty brunette.

"Oh, hi, Ray. Holly, this is my boyfriend, Nick."

Holly's gaze flicked to Jasmine's belly, and she smiled at Nick. "I'm surprised you kept him a secret for so long."

Holly must have assumed they'd been dating since before Jasmine got pregnant. He wouldn't correct anyone who thought that. He tipped his head. "Nice to meet you, Holly. Ray."

"Nick's taking me to lunch, so we'd better go."

Jasmine tugged him past the elevators, and he dragged

his feet a bit. He didn't think anyone had seen him at the wrong end of the hall, but he was nervous about it. She stopped at Rhonda's door and knocked.

"Come in."

He recognized the voice.

Jasmine entered the office and walked up to the desk. "Hi, Rhonda. I want you to meet my boyfriend, Nick."

Rhonda smiled and hugged Jasmine. "I've never had a chance to meet one of your boyfriends before. I guess this one is serious." Her eyes widened on Jasmine's belly. "Really serious."

Jasmine blushed and chuckled nervously. "Yeah, well. I never had a boyfriend before, just event dates. Nick Lawson, Rhonda Whitaker. Rhonda used to be Dad's administrative assistant. Now, she's Uncle Dean's. She knows an amazing amount of information about Kennedy Holdings."

Rhonda's hand opened and closed at her side. Dean's accusation still bothered her. Nick wondered what evidence Dean had fabricated to trap Rhonda. "If you'd been here as long as I've been, you would, too."

Jasmine glanced at him. "Well, we better get going, or we'll miss lunch. Bye, Rhonda."

"Nice meeting you, Rhonda." Now he had a face to go with the woman who had betrayed Jasmine and Josh, and she seemed nervous.

They entered the elevator, and the doors closed. Jasmine leaned against him. "Poor Rhonda. She had a crush on Dad for years. He didn't see it because he never got over Mom."

And now Dean Kennedy was somehow using it against her.

~~~

After Nick dropped Jasmine back at the office, he

realized he didn't have Josh's phone number. He took the chance Josh would be home to tell him about the possible murder of his father. Jasmine hadn't said anything about his getting another job yet.

The door swung open the second time he rang the bell. Josh narrowed his eyes. "Jasmine's not here."

"I know. I just dropped her back at the office after we had lunch. I need to talk to you."

Josh chuckled. "You're not asking for her hand in marriage, are you?"

"No. I'm only asking Jasmine that question. This is something else."

Josh stepped back. "Come on in."

They settled in the living room. Josh leaned back and dropped an arm over the back of the couch. "You have me curious."

"Is Rhonda Whitaker on the board?"

Josh's fingers tapped the couch. "She is. I always thought it was strange that Dad appointed his admin, but she's been there since the dinosaurs. She knows as much about the company as he did."

Nick rubbed the back of his neck. "She helped sway some of the board members to vote against you."

Josh leaned forward. "And you know this how?"

"I took a wrong turn going to Jasmine's office and overheard a conversation between her and Dean."

"So, she sided with him. I wonder why."

"She thought you didn't have enough experience, but that's not the important part."

Josh raised his brows. "What is?"

"She wasn't happy he sold off part of the company, and threatened a new vote. He counter-threatened. He said he'd use his evidence to prove she killed your father."

Josh sprung to his feet. "What! Rhonda killed Dad?"

"Sit!"

Josh dropped onto the couch, and glared.

Nick leaned forward. "She was as shocked as you. I'm guessing your uncle killed your father and has fabricated evidence to implicate Rhonda."

Josh laced his hands on the top of his head. "Oh, my God. I never much liked Uncle Dean. He was a cruel teaser when I was a kid, and I never got over it. But, I can't believe he'd kill his own brother."

"I think we should go to the police with my suspicions. Maybe the hospital still has blood they can check or maybe the body can be exhumed. Some drug must have caused a heart attack."

"Jasmine. This will kill her. I don't think we should tell her until we know for sure Dad was murdered. I don't want her upset over what might turn out to be nothing. She's already been through too much."

Nick nodded. "You're right. We'll wait to tell her. Do you know any detectives?"

"Private detective?"

"Well, I was thinking police, but maybe it would be a good idea to have a private investigator, too."

Josh pulled out his phone. "Dad used to have companies investigated that he was considering buying. They'd be a good place to start."

Josh placed his call and pocketed his phone. "Do you want a drink? I could sure use one."

"All right."

Josh stalked to a sideboard, pulled out two short glasses and poured a couple of fingers of scotch into each. He strode back to Nick and handed him one, then took a swig of his own. He paced then stopped and took a drink. "I can't believe Dad may have been murdered."

The doorbell chimed, and Josh set his glass on the

sideboard then hurried to answer it. A man dressed in a charcoal gray suit followed Josh into the living room. A hint of gray at the temples suggested he was in his late forties.

Nick stood, and the two men stopped in front of him.

"Nick, this is Stuart Banner. Stu, this is Nick Lawson. He's brought something to my attention that I think needs to be checked out. Let's sit."

Nick returned to his chair, and the others sat on the couch.

Josh hunched forward. "Stu, I'm paying for your services. This is not to be discussed with anybody at Kennedy Holdings."

The man squinted and gave a quick nod.

Josh waved toward Nick. "Nick overheard something today that's disturbing." He glanced at Nick. "Why don't you tell it?"

Nick drew in a breath and took several seconds to arrange his thoughts. He repeated, as best he could, the conversation between Rhonda Whitaker and Dean Kennedy.

Stuart rested a hand on the armrest. "I never liked the guy, but I didn't think he had the balls for that." He slid his hands to his knees. "This isn't my area of expertise, so I'll bring in one of our other investigators, Marie Sartog. She's extremely successful at investigating criminal cases. We'll start with hospital records. Was there an autopsy?"

Josh shook his head. "Dad's doctor was sure it was a heart attack."

"Marie will know the steps we have to take to get the body exhumed. You'll have to sign off on it." Stuart stood, and the others followed.

Josh shook Stuart's hand. "I'll do anything to get to the bottom of this. Thanks for coming so quickly. And don't mention anything to Jasmine about this."

"How is Jasmine? I haven't seen her since the funeral. I

kind of miss all her questions about conducting investigations."

Josh grimaced. "Dad's death hit her hard." He dropped his hand on Nick's shoulder. "But this guy has made all the difference."

Nick beamed. With how overprotective Josh was with Jasmine, Nick had been unsure of Josh's opinion of him.

His happiness was overshadowed by this new situation surrounding Jasmine. If her father had been murdered by Dean, what else would he do to ensure he kept control of Kennedy Holdings?

Chapter 9

Jasmine took a pillow from the couch outside and dropped it on the porch. She sat, leaning on the wall of the house, staring at the long expanse of empty space her mother always called a portico. Furniture would have been a nice addition, but whenever she'd asked, her mother always said it was tacky, and she didn't have the heart to change it after her mother's death.

Her mother had loved pouring over gardening magazines and showing her favorite plant pictures to the gardener. It was amazing how he could bring her mother's vague ideas to life. The gardens seemed frozen in time, no one wanted to change the layout.

She tipped her head against the wall and closed her eyes, enjoying the scents of early summer—flowers and flowering bushes—while waiting for Nick's arrival.

At first, she hadn't told Nick about her pregnancy because they might not be together very long, never having been with a guy for more than a couple dates. Then as she started to fall in love with him, she hoped the more time they spent together, the more likely he'd still want to see her once he found out.

Now that Jasmine wasn't worried about his reaction to her pregnancy, she was ready to take the next step in their relationship. If his kisses enflamed her, following through with the rest had to be all consuming. She wanted to explore an intimate relationship with Nick.

She'd fallen in love with him, and he must feel something similar to go to all that trouble to find her.

She rubbed her hand over her stomach. . If he'd been shocked when Josh told him about her pregnancy, he'd hidden it well. He seemed as excited as her about this baby they'd created. It amazed her that, without knowing it, she'd fallen in love with her baby's father.

Something touched her lips, and she startled, her eyes flying open. Nick was inches from her face.

One corner of his mouth tipped up. "Sorry. I couldn't resist." He took her hand and helped her to her feet. "Are you locked out?"

"No. I wanted fresh air while I waited for you." She pointed behind her. "You do know that during the day there's almost always a cook or housekeeper in the house, don't you?"

He laughed. "I'm not used to the way rich people live. It's still weird when someone from the cleaning service comes in once a week."

He backed her into the wall. "Now, let me give you a real kiss." He planted a hand on the wall on each side of her head, and leaned in, his body barely touching her tummy and breasts, as if he was giving her a chance to escape. Her heart fluttered, and her breath came in short bursts. Then his warm lips met hers.

She slid her hands around him and up his back, tangling one hand in his hair. He groaned and pushed closer to her. His mouth slanted over hers and his tongue tickled her lip until she opened for him, then he delved in. She didn't know kisses could be so sexy, and they were doing it on the portico where anyone passing could see. And she didn't care.

He drew back and touched his forehead to hers, giving

them a chance to catch their breaths.

It was a good thing she still leaned against the wall, or her rubbery legs would have given out. She dragged her arms down his back and around to the front, cupping his face. "That was an amazing kiss."

He chuckled, gave her another quick kiss and shoved away. "And it'll be an amazing something else if I don't keep my hands off you. What did you have planned for us?"

She wondered what something else he would have done in semi-public. Locking her knees, she stood tall. "The Bronx Zoo." Inside the front door, she picked up her purse and the overnight bag beside it, and turned back around.

Nick squinted at the bag on her shoulder. "What's that for?"

She bit her lip and stared at a button on his Henley. "It's for going to your place afterward."

He lifted her chin, forcing her to gaze into his eyes. "And what happens at my place?"

She tucked her lip in. "We, um, sleep together. You know." He wasn't making this easy for her.

He raised his brows. "If you can't say it, do you think we should be doing it?"

She huffed out a breath, and drew in another. She wanted it, she could say it. "I want to have sex with you."

He touched his lips to hers. "I want to make love with you." He teased her with another kiss. "We'll reevaluate when we get to my place."

~~~

At the zoo, Nick held Jasmine's hand, setting his gate to her slower one, much slower now than when they'd started the day. He'd made frequent stops on park benches, saying he wanted to watch the monkeys longer, or watch the lion pace—whatever he could come up with to make sure Jasmine rested. Now, their zoo visit was over, and he worried she was too tired to make it back to his car.

He scooped her up and increased his speed. Jasmine wrapped an arm around his neck and held on. "Nick! What are you doing? You can't carry me."

He laughed and kissed her. "I can't? Then what am I doing?"

"I mean, I'm too heavy. You're going to hurt yourself."

"Honey, I carry groceries that weigh more than you." At his car, he lowered his arms, and let her slide down his body, enjoying her amazing body rubbing against his.

He opened the passenger door, and she slipped inside, leaning back and closing her eyes. He rushed to the other side and started the car, turning the air conditioner on high.

Eyes still closed, Jasmine rubbed her hand on his thigh. "Mmm. That air feels good."

He liked her hand on his leg and wished he could move it higher. Not happening yet. He wasn't doing this again when she was only half aware.

"There's a pretty good Chinese restaurant near my apartment. Do you want to pick up take-out and go back to my place?"

"Sounds wonderful."

Nick kissed Jasmine's temple and headed home. She was exhausted with smudges of blue under her eyes. As much as he wanted to make love to her, she'd do better with a good night's sleep.

He turned into the parking garage under his building, waved his pass for the gate to rise then found his designated slot. He got out, rounded the car and opened Jasmine's door. She didn't stir. Maybe she'd stay asleep if he carried her in.

He unbuckled the seatbelt and carefully lifted her from the seat. She snuggled her head into his neck but didn't awaken. At the door, another tenant was leaving and held it open for him, smiling. Nick murmured a thank you.

He managed to hit the buttons to call the elevator and select his floor. He'd kept his keys in his hand, and at his apartment door, he was able to unlock and open it. Inside, he lay Jasmine on the couch, positioned a pillow under her head, and covered her with a throw blanket. She hadn't stirred.

In the kitchen, Nick found the menu for the nearest restaurant and phoned in an order. In the same drawer as the menu, he found a notepad and wrote on the lower half, *Gone for food. Back in a few*. He folded it, writing side out and placed it on the coffee table for Jasmine.

She was still asleep when he returned twenty minutes later. He didn't know if a little over an hour was long enough for a nap. He set out plates and filled a glass with milk for her because pregnant women needed milk, didn't they? After pouring wine for himself, he opened the cartons of food.

In the living room, he sat on the floor in front of Jasmine. He rubbed her hand and spoke softly to her. He wasn't sure how food and sleep worked with pregnancy. Which was more important?

Her eyes fluttered open, and she smiled. "Nick. Mmm. Something smells good."

"I didn't know if I should wake you. Are you hungry?"

She sat up. "I'm famished." She glanced around the room. A crease appeared between her eyebrows. "This is your place?"

He shrugged. "I'm subletting, so it's not my furniture. I still own a house back in Minnesota." It wasn't anything like his own place where the furniture had been chosen for comfort. The stylish pale gray sofa and chairs weren't uncomfortable, but were too formal for his tastes.

He stood, still holding her hand. "Ready to eat?"

"Bathroom first, and then I'm ready."

He drew her up, gave her a kiss, and pointed over his shoulder. "Bathroom's that way."

Nick leaned against the counter in the kitchen, not wanting to sit before Jasmine returned. She stopped in the doorway. He hurried to the table and pulled out a chair. "Have a seat."

Neither spoke as they filled their plates.

He forked and ate a chunk of broccoli as she expertly selected a slice of beef with chopsticks. His parents had rarely brought Chinese food home, and when they did, there were no chopsticks. He'd tried to use them on one of his early trips to New York and given up, preferring to get the food to his mouth.

Jasmine picked up a second piece of meat. "This is fantastic."

He shrugged. "It's the closest place. I lucked out that it's so good."

"Um, Nick." She'd set her chopsticks on her plate, and bit her lip.

He set his fork down, sensing this was important to her.

"I'm having an ultrasound on Wednesday. I thought you might like to come."

He grabbed her hand. "Really? I'd love to."

"It was supposed to be three weeks ago, but I had to cancel. Now, I'm glad I did."

They'd get to see the life they'd made together. Make it more real. He didn't know if that was possible. He already imagined her holding a small baby in her arms, and smiling at him with love.

At the end of the meal, he closed up the cartons.

"Let me help clean up," Jasmine said, and started to rise, but he touched her shoulder.

"No, sit. I'll take care of this." In short order, he put the food in the refrigerator and the dishes in the dishwasher.

He propped a hip on the table. "Do you want to watch a movie?" She still looked tired, so he was pretty sure she'd fall asleep before it was over. He'd fantasized for months about making love to Jasmine again, but he wanted her wide awake and fully participating and that wouldn't happen tonight.

"Okay."

"Why don't you call Josh and tell him you're spending the night?"

Her eyes brightened, and she blushed. "I left him a note."

He chuckled. "I wonder how he reacted to that." He pulled her out of the chair. Knowing how much she wanted him, too, made resisting her one of the hardest things he'd had to do. Her first time remembering making love with him should be crystal clear in her mind. "Why don't you get into your night clothes? I left your bag in my room."

She strolled into his bedroom and he followed, realizing she might have chosen something way to sexy for him to resist. "On second thought, let me see what you brought first."

She unzipped the bag and pulled out a filmy peach confection that wouldn't go halfway to her knees. Not that it would matter how long it was, since the fabric was transparent.

He snatched the wisps from her hand and deposited it on his dresser then found a t-shirt. "You can wear this while we watch the movie."

Jasmine propped her hands on her hips. "But, Nick, I bought that especially for our first time. Um, well, my first time."

He shoved the shirt into her hands. "You can wear it for breakfast, and I'll drool all over my food."

Her mouth dropped open. If things worked out the way he wanted, she'd be well loved by the time they got to breakfast and would be less self-conscious.

Leaving the bedroom, he closed the door and got comfortable on the couch. He selected a few movies, and put them in a folder for Jasmine to choose from.

The opening door caught his attention. Jasmine sauntered toward him. His t-shirt hit halfway to her knees. She'd worn skirts that length, but somehow, in his shapeless shirt, it was sexier. He wondered if she'd kept her panties on. Her unencumbered breasts bounced a bit when she walked. They were larger than the first time he'd been with her. Another thing that should have clued him in she was pregnant.

A handful of steps away, she hesitated. He patted the cushion beside him. "Right here."

She settled in, and he tugged her closer. "I picked out five." He handed her the remote. "Choose whichever you want."

She clicked on the first one, and worked her way through, then backed up one. "*Sherlock Holmes*." She clicked into the movie and set the remote on the table.

He lifted the folded blanket beside him. "Do you want to be covered?"

"Yes. I like to be cozy for movie watching."

Good. He wouldn't have to distract himself from staring at her long, beautiful legs. He tucked the two of them in together.

Thirty minutes in, her body relaxed. He glanced at her, and she gave him a sleepy smile. Another fifteen minutes, and her head rested against his shoulder. He waited a few more minutes and slipped away from her.

In his bedroom, he turned back the bedding then stripped to his boxer briefs. He brushed his teeth, flipped on the night light, and returned to Jasmine. He lifted her with care, making sure not to wake her, although she seemed to be a heavy sleeper.

He set her in the center of the bed and slid in beside her, sharing a pillow. He spooned her, like they'd slept—the little they had—all those months ago.

He rested his hand protectively over her stomach and lightly rubbed it. She was just over five months. He should have read up on the stages of pregnancy. Something fluttered. He sucked in a breath. Was it the baby? He waited, tense. Again.

He rubbed a circle, and whispered. "Hey, little one, time to rest. Don't wake your mom." Mom. In a few months, Jasmine would be a mother, and he would become a father. He'd thought about it before. How could he not when Rob and Ruth had their first baby, and he'd become an uncle?

To feel his baby's movements under his hand made it real. Already, their child was as important to him as Jasmine.

He nuzzled her neck, and kissed it. "I love you."

She wiggled tighter into him. Perfect.

Chapter 10

Jasmine awakened with a warm body at her back. Her eyes popped open. A strange room. She scanned as far as she could without moving, and relaxed. Nick's bedroom. She'd changed here last night. It wasn't like the last time she'd woken in a strange bed in Nick's hotel room, not knowing who was in the other room.

Nick. The last thing she remembered was watching a movie with him. After she'd fallen asleep, he must have carried her to his room.

His arm tightened around her, and he kissed below her ear. It sent a delicious shiver through her torso. He responded by nudging the hardest part of him against her backside.

"Good. You're awake. Last time, I made the mistake of leaving the bed before you woke."

What would have happened if he'd still been in bed and awake when she opened her eyes all those months ago? She probably would have been too embarrassed and run anyway.

Not this time. She squirmed around until she faced him. Sort of. She stared at his neck. "Good morning."

He lifted her chin until their gazes met. "Morning." He kissed her nose. "You look refreshed. Ready for all kinds of strenuous activities?" Oh, that smile told her of the kinds of activities he wanted.

Her traitorous cheeks warmed. "Um, I need to use the

bathroom before any kind of activities."

He lifted the blanket. "I'll be waiting here for you."

She scurried to the bathroom and relieved her full bladder. If she'd been awake when she'd gone to bed, she would have her toothbrush in here. She not only had morning breath, it was yesterday breath, too. Inside the mirrored cabinet, she found mouthwash, and swished a little. Nick had a comb, but there was no way she could get that through her hair. Finger combing would have to do.

Now she was ready. Maybe. It seemed like butterflies held her feet to the floor. She sucked in two deep breaths. She'd wanted this for a while, but didn't know what to expect. For Nick, it wasn't their first time.

His voice penetrated the door. "Jasmine, are you okay?"

Another deep breath and the butterflies released her feet. She opened the door and strode to the bed, then froze, biting her lip.

Nick was propped up on his side, his elbow under him, his naked chest exposed. The covers pooled around his waist, so she didn't know if the rest of him was naked. She liked his chest. It was muscular, but not bulky like a weightlifter. A sprinkling of hair drew her eyes down to where it disappeared under the blankets. And she'd touched all this before. She snapped her gaze back to his eyes, and her breath caught at the love gleaming in them. There'd been times she caught men admiring her as if they were stripping her and this was nothing like that.

He folded the covers back. "Come, join me." It wasn't a command, more like an appeal.

She sat on the bed with her back to him. His arm wrapped around her waist and dragged her to his chest. His breath tickled her neck when he spoke. "Do you still want to make love? We don't have to. We can get dressed and have breakfast."

She leaned into him and tipped her head back, nestling it into his neck. Nothing felt as right as being in his arms. "I want to. I'm just nervous. Do we just…do it?"

He kissed her temple. "Oh, no. There's lots before that. First we start with kisses."

He laid back, his muscled chest tight against her, and she twisted to face him. Her breath caught at the expression in his eyes. He wanted this as much as she did. His confidence calmed her nerves, only to be replaced with a mounting excitement.

Jasmine remembered her hand running up a chest—his chest. She'd done all kinds of unremembered things in a bed with this man. All those months ago, her plan must have been to use him to forget her loss for a while. Wonderful Nick had never mentioned her selfishness. The connection they'd shared—even before having sex—had urged him to find her.

She stared into those beautiful, dark eyes. Eyes she could gaze into forever. She tipped closer, and closer until their lips touched. His hand slid up her neck, threaded into the back of her hair, and he took over the kiss. His lips were always warmer than hers, but it didn't take long for the temperature of hers to match, and the rest of her followed.

His tongue tantalized her, reminding her how it had affected her the morning before. She opened for him, and he groaned as he rolled her to her back and kissed her deeper. He somehow encouraged her tongue to delve into his mouth.

Before Nick, the thought of this kind of kiss had held such a high yuck factor, she didn't think she'd ever do it. Not with all those cardboard dates, most of whom she'd turned her head and gotten a kiss on the cheek. She wouldn't have shared a fork with them. With Nick, she craved that kind of intimacy.

She wrapped an arm around his waist and ran her hand up his rippling ribs. She grazed her nails up his neck and into his hair. He moaned. She'd done that to him, and it excited her to have an effect.

He must have taken her touching him as an invitation to explore her. His fingers caressed her leg just above her knee, and brushed up, slipping under the edge of the t-shirt. Before Nick, she'd never had fantasies. There was that vague someday-she'd-have-sex, but now her dreams were filled with touching Nick—running her hands over his washboard abs, kissing so intimately her breath quickened, and faltering before his pants came off. After today, her fantasies would be complete.

All her senses had been tied into his kisses. Now, she had a new focus. His hand crept higher and anticipation left her gasping. She threw back her head to catch her breath. It didn't work. His lips traveled across her jaw, and down her neck. Warm, pleasurable shivers overtook her, and she moaned.

The shirt shifted under her butt. The breath from his whisper sent another shiver through her. "Let's get this off you."

Perfect idea. She lifted her upper body and the shirt was gone in seconds. Before the air could cool her, his warm kisses circled a breast. He suckled her nipple, and her hand clenched in his hair. The new sensations raging through her made her want more.

"Nick!"

He kissed her neck. "You okay, honey?"

"Yes. I need more!"

"That's what I was thinking."

He slipped her panties under her and off her legs. Then he nudged her legs apart and settled between them. One hand snaked up to her breast and his fingers wrapped around it before his thumb rubbed across her nipple. Her breath sawed in and out in short bursts. Then he slipped down, kissing a trail along her ribs and over her stomach until his mouth found her. The intensity swamped her, and she intended to push him away, but when her hands gripped the sides of his head, she held it there. Dizziness overtook her and a tingly pressure built low inside her. Maybe she was hyperventilating. If so, she'd never appreciated it like she did now.

Pleasurable pulses consumed her and she screamed, jamming the bottoms of her feet into the sides of Nick's ribs. Finally, her breathing slowed with only the occasional earthquake aftershock.

She jumped when he rose up and nudged her opening, and her eyes flew open. He kissed her, and she tasted herself on his lips—another thing she thought would have been distasteful, but sharing it with Nick made her want more of them.

"You ready for this?" He studied her. Even though he hadn't had an orgasm yet, he'd stop if she wasn't ready.

She was *so* ready to find out everything she'd blocked out from her first time and nodded. Her voice was a scratchy whisper. "Yes."

He kissed her. He slid in a little and retreated. It took a couple of times to notice he synchronized with his tongue. This was more intense than anything she'd imagined. She curled her legs around him, and he surged in. She gasped and held him tighter. He buried his head in her neck and nibbled.

"Yes!" She said that? It all felt so good.

His tempo increased, and her body tightened, intensifying the pleasure. He reached between them, touching her where his lips had been, and she screamed as her world shattered. His hand on her arm tightened, then he surged forward, stiffening, and an almost roar left his lips.

It took time to get their breathing under control—as if they'd run a race. One she wouldn't mind running again, and again, and again.

Nick lay half on her, just enough weight to remind her of what they'd shared. His arm circled her.

She felt protected. "I can't believe I didn't remember last time. That was…wow. Better than anything I've ever done."

He chuckled and kissed her cheek. "I agree."

She tipped her head away from him, and frowned. She didn't want to think about him with other women but… "I'm inexperienced. Surely, other women would know how to give you more pleasure."

He slowly shook his head. "There's more to it than that. We made love." He kissed her. "I love you, Jasmine. That makes this special."

Her smile trembled, and she couldn't stop the tears. Stupid pregnancy hormones. Had their first time been just sex? She couldn't ask that, not wanting to hear the answer. She touched his face. "I love you, too."

He swooped down for a kiss. "Let's shower, and I'll make you breakfast."

"Okay. You go first and—"

"Nope. Together. I don't want you disappearing on me like last time."

"I won't—"

He smirked. "I'm teasing." He stood, and she got a full view of his nakedness. His eyes were crinkled in merriment by the time her gaze landed on his face and warmth spread across her cheeks.

He took her hand and gently pulled her up against him. "I'm glad you decided to spend the night."

"Me, too." After she found out she was pregnant, she hadn't expected to find a man who would love her and her baby. Nick was a dream come true.

Chapter 11

Nick rubbed his eyes and rested his head against the back of the seat in the cab. He hated redeye flights, but he needed to get back to Jasmine.

He'd had to make an emergency trip back to Minnesota on Monday to take care of business. Since he was there, and Independence Day was only two days away, his mother had invited him to their cookout. He hadn't seen his parents or Tricia, in months, so he couldn't refuse. His sister had brought a date. He seemed like a nice guy—better than her ex.

Nick was happy he'd stayed when Rob and Ruth made a surprise visit. He got to see how much Emily had grown and meet little Jackson. His niece was the spitting image of her mother and would be a heartbreaker someday.

After debating, he'd decided it was a good time to tell everybody about Jasmine, and that he was going to be a father. He fudged a bit when they asked how he'd met her, telling them about the auction.

They were happy for him, but his mother gave him that look meaning he wasn't setting a good example. In this instance, he was following in Rob's footsteps. He and Ruth had married after she got pregnant, although they'd already been engaged.

He checked his watch. He should get to Jasmine's office

fifteen minutes before they had to leave for her appointment. There was no way he'd miss seeing his baby in the ultrasound.

With the crash of metal ahead of them and honking horns, traffic froze. No! Okay, he could do this. He was only four blocks from Jasmine's office. He'd walk. It didn't matter if he was hot and sweaty when he got there, the important thing was making it to the appointment.

He yanked out his wallet and tossed money at the taxi driver. "Here."

He leapt from the car, and wove through stopped cars to the sidewalk. As always, the walks were as packed as the streets. His pace wasn't nearly as fast as he wanted. He darted around a large man in a gray suit as the man waved his arm, hitting Nick in the shoulder. Nick grunted, but kept going.

He approached the right turn as a gap opened, and he slid into it, speeding up for a dozen feet, only to come up on a wall of people. There was another gap ahead of them, but no way around.

Nick turned sideways and jostled between two people. "Excuse me."

An orange pedestrian light at the corner ahead had him cursing. People already stood at least six deep at the corner. He angled down the side street, and stopped at the curb, waiting for a break in traffic or the light to flash *WALK*. He checked the time and found Jasmine would be leaving in five minutes.

The light changed and Nick jogged between stopped cars, ending up between waves of crowds. He broke into a run and darted around a mother holding her toddler's hand, bumping the man ahead of her as he squeezed between him and a wall, only then noticing the white cane. Jeez. He'd almost knocked over a blind guy. "Sorry."

He grabbed another opening and raced ahead. Nick glanced at his watch half a block from Jasmine's building to find he was five minutes late. Then he saw her.

"Jasmine!"

She opened the cab door and slipped inside.

"No!" He shoved a man aside and raced, glad for a narrow passage. He slammed into the side of the cab. "Wait!"

Jasmine's eyes widened, and her muffled voice penetrated the glass. "Stop!" She opened the door, and scooted back.

Nick dropped in beside her. "Thanks."

She gripped his hand. "Nick, I waited as long as possible, but I can't be late for this appointment."

He kissed her and fell back, still catching his breath. "I planned on being early, but there was an accident. I decided it would be faster if I ran. I forgot about all the foot traffic." He cupped her cheek. "I wouldn't miss this for anything."

She pulled his hand down, but didn't let go. "How was your family?"

As soon as he'd accepted his mother's invitation, he'd called to tell Jasmine why he was delayed, and they'd talked for over an hour. "Good. Rob and Ruth made a surprise visit with the kids."

"It's great you all got to be together. How often do you see them?"

He rubbed his head. "At least one of them, every few months, but all together? I don't know. Maybe two years?" He leaned in and kissed her, then kept his eyes on hers. "I told them about you and the baby."

She bit her lip. "They were okay with it? They don't think I'm—"

He grinned. "They were ecstatic." His expression softened. "I told them about meeting you at the charity auction." He glanced away and back to her. "I couldn't quite bring myself to tell them I took a drunken woman to my hotel room."

The driver snorted, and Jasmine's gaze darted toward him. He'd forgotten about the cabby.

He squeezed her hand. "If any of them check out the ball, they'll know the baby timetable is off, but I didn't want to put you in that position."

She shrugged one shoulder. "If they find out, they find out. I'm not regretting it now."

"I'm sorry you had regrets."

She rubbed a hand over her little bump. "I never regretted this, only that I didn't know who the baby's father was." She tickled his ear with her lips. "And maybe a little that I don't remember our first time."

He whispered back. "There'll be so many times, it won't matter."

She kept her voice low. "Maybe you'll have to tell me about the first."

"I don't know. It would almost feel like I was telling you about me having sex with another woman." Drunken Jasmine had been so wanton and open, he'd had no idea it was her first time, until it was too late. It might be some time before Jasmine would feel uninhibited with him. He anticipated it.

The cab swerved and stopped in front of the building doors. "Here you go, folks."

Nick gave the man a couple of bills and ushered Jasmine from the cab. He glanced up at the tall structure. "Do you know where we're going?"

Jasmine took his hand. "Yes. It's on the second floor."

He followed her into the elevator, up to the reception desk and to padded chairs in the waiting area.

She grabbed his hand and flattened it over the side of her stomach. "I think the baby is as excited as I am."

He waited and a flutter crossed his palm. Even though

he'd felt it before, it carried the same thrill. He grinned. "We've already been introduced."

She raised her brows.

"When I put you to bed, I snuggled up behind you with my hand on your belly. The baby kicked and I told him, or her, to let you sleep."

A door swung open, and a woman in scrubs with a messy bun called out. "Jasmine Kennedy?"

They approached, and stopped in front of her.

"Jasmine?"

"Yes."

"I'm Chandra. This way." The woman turned and Jasmine followed with him close on her heels. The woman entered a small room and patted a paper-covered table. "Up here."

Jasmine could have gotten up herself, but Nick lifted her into place and gave her a quick kiss. She lay on her back with her head on a pillow.

Chandra turned dials and depressed buttons, then slipped on surgical gloves. "Now, lift your shirt and push down your waistband."

Nick admired her beautiful belly. He couldn't help himself. He leaned down and kissed it. Jasmine giggled as he took her hand.

Chandra picked up a bottle. "Lucky thing he kissed you before I smeared this gel on your belly."

Jasmine's eyes sparkled. "Dr. Connors uses that when we listen to the baby's heartbeat."

She'd heard the baby before. Nick had missed something already.

She squirted gel over Jasmine's skin.

"Oh, it's not cold."

Chandra laughed. "Yeah, we heat it."

"I wish Dr. Connors did."

Chandra held the device against Jasmine's stomach. "We'll start with listening." A swishing beat filled the room, as the woman checked her watch.

Nick's gaze met Jasmine's and she smiled. He squeezed her hand and returned the smile.

The woman pulled the instrument away, silencing their baby's heartbeat. She cleaned the device, and made a note on the chart.

She picked up a transducer and smeared gel on it, then placed it against Jasmine's stomach.

"Now, the main attraction," Chandra said. She slid the device around. "There's the baby's head."

Jasmine squealed. "Look at the little nose!"

Nick tore his eyes from their child to watch Jasmine's face glow with wonder.

"Oh, and little tiny fingers. Look! He's wiggling them." Her eyes shimmered with tears.

It wasn't just snapshots. The baby moved, kicking a leg out, turning the head. His heart swelled with love for this baby he wouldn't be able to hold for months.

Chandra slid her transducer to a new spot. "There's a thigh."

"Is the baby too thin?" Nick didn't want anything to be wrong with their child.

"No. Everything's fine. Babies put on the most weight in their last month. Now let's see if we can find out the baby's sex."

The view changed as Chandra shifted the transducer. The baby kicked and Nick couldn't hold in a laugh.

The view changed again. "There you go. You have yourself a boy."

"A son." He kissed Jasmine. "We have a son." A boy who would be a protector of little sisters. Yes. He wanted more children with Jasmine.

Chandra ran a damp cloth around Jasmine's tummy. "All done." She reached behind her, and picked up a couple of pictures and a CD, which she slid into a sleeve. "Here you go, Dad."

He thought he'd already accepted impending fatherhood, but to hear it like that. Wow! He froze for a couple seconds before taking the package from the woman, then grinned.

He led Jasmine out of the office and backed her into an alcove. "I love you. It means a lot to me you're having our baby." He gave her a tender kiss, like one of their early ones.

"I never considered getting rid of my baby, but I assumed I'd be alone in raising him. I knew Josh would make a wonderful uncle, but he'll get married some day and have his own family."

"I'll be here for both of you. Marry me, Jasmine." He'd intended to propose on bended knee in a romantic setting when the time was right, but seeing their baby, he couldn't put it off.

Her eyes widened, and she sucked in a breath. "Yes!" She threw her arms around his neck.

He hugged her with their growing child between. He'd hoped to have a loving relationship one day similar to his parents' and brother's, but never expected such an all-consuming love. Nearly every decision he'd made since meeting Jasmine had been with her in mind. She and their child would always be his priority.

Chapter 12

Two days after the ultrasound appointment, Nick parked in front of the Kennedy mansion. Josh asked Nick to join him for lunch without giving him any idea what they'd discuss. It couldn't be about his relationship with Jasmine since he'd taken responsibility for the baby, but they hadn't talked since she'd spent the night at his place.

Josh opened the door before the chimes of the doorbell finished. "Come on in."

He led Nick to the dining room, where two places were set. It was relatively small as far as mansion rooms went, so he assumed there was a larger, formal dining room nearby. As soon as they were seated, an older woman bustled in with a large tray. She set a tureen of a creamy soup between them, and glass-covered dishes holding asparagus with hollandaise sauce, and steak tips with onions.

Even covered, the dishes smelled heavenly. "Quite the spread for lunch."

Josh shrugged. "Usually, I make myself a couple of sandwiches, but hey, I've got a guest." He gestured at the tureen. "Help yourself."

Nick ladled the creamy soup into his bowl. Nick had eaten half his soup when Josh set down his spoon. Whatever he said next would be the reason for this get-together.

Josh tapped a couple of fingers on the table. "I heard

back from my investigator on the autopsy."

It had been about three weeks since Nick had told Josh what he'd overheard.

Josh picked up his spoon and stirred his soup, staring into it. "There was alcohol and a large quantity of amphetamines in his system. Dad didn't do drugs. Stuart had the reports turned over to the police, and they've opened a case for suspicious death." Pain pinched his features. "Thanks for telling me what you overheard. His death shouldn't go unpunished."

Nick couldn't imagine learning something like this about someone he loved. A death that shouldn't have happened. Someone, probably Josh's uncle, selfishly took another man's life.

"Glad to help. I'm sorry it turned out this way."

"Me, too." Josh's voice cracked. "He would have still been with us."

There was nothing Nick could say to make this better. Jasmine would be just as hurt.

Josh rubbed a hand over his face. "I have to tell her. The police are involved now. I don't want her to hear about this from anyone else." Josh sighed and set aside his soup bowl. He opened the covered dishes and served himself steak, onions and asparagus.

Nick followed suit.

Josh cut a piece of steak. "What are your intentions with my sister?"

He chuckled, expecting this question long before now. "I intend to be married to her before the baby's born."

Josh lifted an eyebrow. "She hasn't told me you're engaged."

"I asked her the day of the ultrasound. I'm surprised she hasn't told you yet, but I still have to get a ring. I was thinking of a wedding in Minnesota near my folks. I'll want my family there, and you, of course. I'd fly out anybody she wants."

"I wouldn't wait too much longer if I were you. You've only got about three months."

~~~

Jasmine squinted at Josh. He fidgeted and pushed the food around on his plate. So far, she'd eaten more food than he had. Lydia had prepared a wonderful dinner, and would be disappointed Josh didn't do it justice.

"Then I told Holly you'd kiss her senseless the next time you saw her, and she was all for it."

Josh continued cutting his pork roast into tiny pieces. "Yeah, okay."

She slammed her fork onto the table. "Josh! You didn't even hear me."

"Of course, I did."

She tipped her head. "What did I say?"

"You were talking to Holly."

She nodded. "And what did I tell her?"

"You said…" He shrugged. "I don't know."

She tried not to smile, but a bit of one escaped. "That you'd kiss her senseless when you saw her."

His eyes widened, and his fork clattered to his plate. "What?"

Jasmine giggled. "No, I didn't, but I think you should do it."

"She's too young for me."

Jasmine noticed he didn't say he didn't want to kiss Holly. "You're only seven years older."

"Which is like a canyon. She's only twenty-two."

"*She* doesn't think you're too old. She's always asking how you're doing. I think she misses you."

He narrowed his eyes. She smiled. Seed planted.

She slid her plate away. "Now, tell me what's bothering you."

"How do you know something's bothering me?"

She rolled her eyes, and pointed to his plate. "How often do you leave that much food at the end of a meal?"

He glanced at his plate. "Well, at least yours is practically empty, and it wouldn't have been if I'd already told you." He stood. "Come on. Let's go to the living room."

She followed, dreading what he had to say. If he thought she wouldn't be able to eat, it had to be bad. He waited for her to sit, and he settled beside her, taking her hand.

Really bad.

His sad eyes stared at her. "I had Dad's body exhumed for an autopsy."

She jerked her hand, but he didn't let go. "What?! Why?"

"Nick overheard a conversation that was suspicious. It turned out to be right. There were alcohol and amphetamines in his system."

"No! You know he didn't take drugs." Tears stung her eyes and overflowed.

Josh trapped her hand between his. "Jasmine, the two together are a deadly combination. It can mimic a heart attack or stroke. Someone did this to him."

"Who would do that to Dad? Everybody liked him."

"Somebody thought things would be better without him."

Jasmine's heart ached. She choked on her words. "I'm not better without him."

Josh hauled her into a hug. "I'm not, either. All we can do is let justice take care of the culprit."

"Who do you think did it?"

"The police are investigating."

She nodded against his chest, noticing he hadn't answered her actual question. He likely knew, but wasn't telling her. "He'd still be with us."

If their dad was still alive, they'd still have his jokes, his smiles, his training of Josh and her. Uncle Dean wouldn't have been in a position to sell off a piece of the company. And she never would have met Nick and gotten pregnant with his baby.

She wished she could have all of the men she loved.

~~~

Nick mulled for a couple weeks who would be his proxy at the board of directors meetings. He would have chosen Alex, except Jasmine had met him. He wanted to be an anonymous company until his proxy was accepted on the board. His representative would get better results if no one knew the new owner had a connection with a Kennedy. In the end, he chose his director of sales. Matt could stand out in a crowd or hide in it. At Kennedy Holdings, he'd have to do both.

Ten o'clock. It was one of his work-at-home days. Matt would likely be at the office.

"Lawson Prime Secure, Matt Dunbar speaking."

"Hey, Matt. It's Nick. Are you free for lunch?"

"Oh, hi, Nick. Yeah, I had a client cancel this morning."

Normally, Nick would ask who the client was and if he needed to give a call. Right now, his only thoughts were of Kennedy Holdings. "Can you meet me at *Freddy's* at noon?" It was two blocks from the office. Nick could catch a cab and make it in twenty-five minutes.

"I'll be there."

"Thanks." Nick hung up before Matt could ask anything more.

He'd picked a short project that didn't require intense concentration knowing he'd have to drag his attention back to the work at hand. Nick worked on coding until it was time to leave.

He closed the laptop, grabbed his keys and went out to flag down a taxi.

The section of the city near his office, like so many others, had a mix of residences and businesses. He hadn't tried most of the restaurants they passed, but *Freddy's American Eatery* had become a favorite. It served simple food quickly.

It was five minutes to noon. Matt approached, his blond head towered over the three women walking in front of him. Nick caught the slim, six-foot-three man's blue eyes, and nodded. Matt worked his way to the edge of the crowd and stepped out beside Nick.

Nick gestured for Matt to precede him into the restaurant, and they were immediately seated.

The server arrived. "Can I start you with something to drink?"

The men ordered drinks and specialty burgers. "I'll get that right in." With a swish of her ponytail, she was gone.

The server returned shortly with their beers, and Matt took a couple gulps. "Do you want a sales update?"

"No. This isn't about work. Well, not ours."

Matt lowered his brows. "You've got me mystified."

Nick scanned the room, not wanting the wrong person to overhear. "I bought into Kennedy Holdings and need to put someone on the board."

"Whoa! Kennedy Holding? That must have cost you a lot."

Nick grimaced. "More than I wanted to spend. I have to remain anonymous for now, so I need a proxy to take my place on the board."

Matt pointed at his chest. "Me? You want me on the board of a billion dollar company? I don't know the first thing about how they work."

"You've done presentations to the heads of billion dollar corporations. You'll be comfortable with this group. You'll get an agenda before each meeting. I think they only have one a quarter. We can go over strategies so you know where I stand. Mostly, I want you to get a feel for each of the other members, and find out if they support Dean Kennedy, the current CEO."

Matt drummed his fingers on the table. "You want me to spy?"

Nick shifted back in his seat. "Sort of." He hadn't thought of it like that. It was a way to gain information to get Josh back in control, especially now that it was likely Dean had killed his own brother.

The server arrived with their plates. She set one in front of him. "The southwestern." She set a burger before Matt. "The Italian. Can I get you anything else?"

Nick glanced at Matt's half full glass. "We're good. Thanks."

Nick couldn't get a read on Matt, which was a good thing because the board wouldn't be able to either. "So, what do you say?"

Matt tipped his head. "Obviously, this is important to you."

Nick nodded. "Of course, you'll be compensated for holding the position and for any meetings you attend."

"How are you keeping anonymous besides not being on the board?"

"I created a new company to buy in. Prime Properties. If someone dug into it, they could find me, but it doesn't need to be kept secret for more than a few months."

Matt stretched his arm across the table. "All right. I'll do it."

Nick shook his hand. "Thanks. I'll let you know when the first meeting is set up."

Chapter 13

Nick's heart fluttered, and he took two quick breaths. His nervousness took him by surprise. He'd already proposed to Jasmine and gotten her answer. Tonight, he'd do it right with a ring. He seemed to have a habit of doing things wrong the first time with Jasmine. He plucked the small box from his pocket and peeked inside. It had been two weeks since he'd proposed, but it had taken time to find the right ring.

He hadn't chosen the most expensive because Jasmine wouldn't want to wear a monstrosity. The third jeweler he'd visited had shown him several trays of rings, and his eyes kept returning to this one. Two pear-shaped diamonds bracketed the round center stone with small diamonds circling the band. He hoped she liked it.

He tucked the box in his pocket and rang the doorbell. The door opened, and Jasmine's gorgeous smile took his breath away. Chance had brought them together and helped him find her again. He couldn't imagine going back to his life before her.

Nick had told her that morning he was taking her to *Giorgio's*, so she would know to dress up. Her jade green gown hugged her breasts and her beautiful belly. She could be the perfect model for maternity clothes—graceful and stylish.

He took her hands and kissed her cheek. "You are

ravishing."

She smiled and brushed a kiss across his lips.

He was so thankful he'd found her both times. "You ready to go?"

Her gaze darted over his shoulder, and her eyes widened. "A limo?"

"I didn't want anything to distract me from you tonight, and I didn't want you to wait for a cab." He led her to the car, and the driver opened the door. She slid across the seat and he followed.

She snuggled into his side. "I haven't been in a limo since…" Her hand flew to her mouth, and her eyes filled with tears. "Since Josh and I lost the company."

Nick pulled her closer. "Oh, honey. I wouldn't have rented it if I'd realized it would make you sad." He'd seen that video on the news and never considered how it would affect her. She might have even ridden in a limo for her father's funeral.

Jasmine rested her head on his shoulder. "Sorry. It's the pregnancy hormones. I wouldn't have expected to react this way, either." She bunched his lapel in her fist. "Josh told me Dad was murdered. The police are investigating." She took a shuddering breath. "He said you overheard something. Why didn't you tell me?"

"Josh didn't want you getting upset over nothing if the autopsy came back as no foul play."

Nick plucked a tissue from a box in the console and dabbed at her cheeks. She bit her lip and finished drying her face. Josh must not have told her everything, or she would have mentioned Dean. It wasn't his place to tell her.

He kissed the top of her head. "I'm sorry, honey." He'd wanted to make the evening perfect, and it was spoiled before reaching the restaurant.

She'd regained her composure by the time the car

stopped in front of *Giorgio's*. The driver opened the door, and handed Nick a card.

"Call when you're ready for pickup. I'll be a block or two away."

"Thanks." Nick slipped it in his pocket. His heart rate kicked up when he ran his fingers over the ring box.

The hostess showed them to his reserved table outside in a dim corner with a view of the harbor.

Nick sat next to Jasmine at a round table, both facing the water, and holding her hand in her lap. Her beautiful face took on a golden glow in the setting sun. The tension between her eyes eased as her gaze settled on the sailboats coming in before the fall of darkness.

After their drinks were served, a coke for him and mineral water with lemon for Jasmine, the server took dinner orders. It would have been nice to drink something stronger with dinner, but Jasmine abstained, so he did as well. Besides, he didn't want anything clouding his mind when he presented her with the ring and proposed a second time.

Jasmine opened her mouth to speak, but her eyes widened. "Give me your hand."

He let her take it, and she flattened it to the side of her belly. An erratic pulse beat against his palm, stronger than previous times. Their little champ was growing bigger and stronger.

He grinned. The ultrasound scans made the baby real, but each time he felt his son move, his love for their child increased. In only a few months, they'd be parents.

The kicking stopped, and he rubbed in a circle, hoping to get a reaction.

"Here we go." The server set a basket of bread on the table, and placed their glasses in front of them. "Would you like an appetizer?"

They declined and placed their orders then she left.

Jasmine dragged his hand to the other side. "He moved. He's not usually this active at dinner time. It happens more often when I'm trying to fall asleep."

It was special and exciting for him but had probably become a nuisance for Jasmine when she needed sleep. "I'm sorry."

She placed her hand over his. "I'm not. It's kind of reassuring to feel him move as I drift off to sleep."

"When's your next doctor's appointment?"

"Day after tomorrow."

"Can I come?"

Her eyebrows rose. "You want to come to a regular appointment?"

"Sure. We get to hear the heartbeat again, right?"

"Yes."

"Perfect. And I can get an update on your and the baby's health."

Dinner arrived. Conversation jumped from topic to topic. Jasmine always had interesting perspectives.

Nick was relieved he'd already asked Jasmine the most important question of his life and had her answer. If he'd taken the time to think it through, he would have been a nervous wreck. But she deserved a better proposal than one given in a hospital corridor.

The server cleared the dishes, and Nick ordered chocolate mousse for dessert.

Jasmine rubbed her tummy. "I don't know if I have room for dessert."

He squeezed her hand. "We'll split it." She wouldn't be able to resist a couple of bites.

Jasmine chuckled. "A forkful or two."

A couple minutes later the server returned. "Here we go." She set a plate between them and added fresh forks. "Enjoy."

Nick stared down at the plate, wondering if Jasmine would go first for the squiggly whipped cream at the sides or the mousse.

She scooped a small chunk of creamy mousse into her mouth then closed her eyes. "Mmm. This is so good."

He couldn't resist. He leaned in and kissed a bit of chocolate off her lip.

She startled and her eyes flew open.

He followed with a kiss. "I love you, Jasmine."

A smile touched her lips, and she leaned in and kissed him. "I love you, too."

He took her hand. "The more time I spend with you, the more I love you. Jasmine, please marry me."

Her eyes twinkled in merriment. "Nick, I already said yes. Didn't you believe me?"

"I do believe you, but this is how I planned to ask you, and I ruined it by proposing in a hallway."

"It wasn't ruined." She touched his chest over his heart. "It was extra special because you couldn't hold in how much you love the baby and me."

He covered her hand on his chest. "Just to be clear, I loved you before I found out about our baby."

Her eyes misted, and she blinked, giving a nod. "I know."

He fished the box from his pocket, and lifted the ring from its bed, then slid it onto her finger. A perfect fit.

She gasped. "Nick, it's beautiful. How did you guess my ring size?"

Nick grinned. "I had Josh take one of yours so I could size your engagement ring. I didn't want there to be any reason for you to take it off."

Her gaze dropped to her ringed hand. "Nick, I wouldn't mind if we left now and got to the other dessert."

He sucked in a breath. Yeah, he wouldn't mind that

either. Their server was at another table, and he gestured for the check. She nodded.

He couldn't contain his happiness. He was sure he glowed as much as Jasmine did. It felt more official with the ring on her finger. Soon, she'd be his wife, and nothing compared to that.

~~~

Jasmine threw down her pen, got up and paced. The board was meeting for the first time since part of the company had been sold. She was intent on meeting the new member and sizing them up. Maybe they could become friends and she could find out what was happening.

Fifteen more minutes. She stopped at her desk and took a long drink of mineral water with lemon, then resumed her pacing. She really should get more work done, but her mind had wandered from the moment she arrived. At least, she was getting exercise. By the time the meeting started, she probably would have walked a mile.

Thirteen minutes. Time moved too slowly. The stairs. She'd climb up a few floors and come back down. Out the door she headed for the stairs beside the elevator, passing no one at her end of the hall. She thrust the door open and climbed. Two floors up, she paused to catch her breath. She'd forgotten her pregnancy would make the climb difficult. She leaned against the wall until her breathing slowed.

She'd probably be sweaty meeting the new board member. Hopefully, a stop at the restroom would fix that. She hurried down the stairs, her hand skimming the railing. She couldn't chance a misstep causing her to tumble.

At the second floor landing, a man noticed her and paused. He stepped aside.

"Thanks, but I'm going in here." She waved her hand at

the door.

"Me, too. Maybe you can make sure I get to the conference room."

He had to be the new board member. He was younger than she expected—taller than her by a head, and thin. She wondered if he had purchased the ten-percent or if he'd been appointed by that person.

His blue eyes darted to her stomach and back to her face. He stuck his hand out. "Matt Dunbar."

She shook it. "Jasmine Kennedy."

He grinned. "One of the owners of the company?"

"It doesn't feel like it." If they hadn't had board members, Josh would still be the CEO.

"Ah. The board controls the company, so it doesn't feel like yours."

"Pretty much. Especially when the board makes decisions I don't agree with." Getting rid of Josh. Selling a portion of Kennedy Holdings to this man.

"Well hopefully, my influence will be more to your liking." He opened the door. "Shall we?"

She hoped he wasn't trying to befriend her because she was an owner of the company, although he seemed nice enough. Maybe he could influence some of the other board members as he said.

"All right. Let me introduce you."

His hand still held the door. "Are you attending the meeting?"

She shook her head. "No. I've been barred. But I can introduce you before I leave."

His eyebrows shot up, and he released the door, allowing it to close. "You're barred? You want me to try to change that?"

Her breath caught. "You'd do that? I don't want you to cause yourself trouble. Maybe let it slide until next time."

He frowned. "All right. I won't mention it this time, but you should be in there. Even if you can't vote."

That's what she thought. She'd had voting rights before Uncle Dean took over. Since Josh already had voting right, she'd assumed her father's. And then she and Josh were both kicked out.

Matt leaned against the wall. "Do you want me to stop by your office afterward and tell you about it?"

She bit her lip. "It might get you in trouble with some of the other board members. Besides, why would you do that for me?"

"I've done my homework and read up on the firm." He nodded toward the door. "I'm not going in there to make friends. I'll be friendly enough, but my votes won't be influenced by any of them." He yanked the door open.

Jasmine didn't know what he learned, but hoped it was in her and Josh's favor. She led him to the conference room. He wasn't at all what she'd expected—an old man who would try to befriend the board, then subtly coerce them into doing what he wanted. Matt seemed like he would be open in whatever he planned to do.

Jasmine lifted her head and strode into the conference room as if she owned it. And she did own a share of it, but none of these people treated her like that. She got outright glares from some of the long time members. Sweet Rhonda smiled, always in Jasmine's corner.

She took another sweeping view of the members, one group of three and the other of four. Uncle Dean was absent. Jasmine cleared her throat. "Good morning. I ran into your newest board member on the stairs. This is Matt Dunbar." She started on the left, reciting everyone's name. By the time she finished, Dean had arrived. "And this is Dean Kennedy, CEO of Kennedy Holdings."

Her uncle gave her a saccharine smile. "Jasmine, you

know you're not supposed to attend the board meeting."

Only because he insisted on it. "Yes, I know, Uncle Dean. I ran into Matt and offered to show him to the conference room. I'll leave you to your meeting."

She scanned the group once more, only finding sympathy in Rhonda's and Matt's eyes. She hoped someday the board would recognize the founder's children as equals.

Chapter 14

Nick had studied years of financials for Kennedy Holdings, and his calculations showed more than enough earnings to cover his bank loan for the purchase. Either Dean was steering the company into ruin or he was skimming. Nick would have Matt request a copy of the company's most recent financials.

This first check didn't cover his bank loan payment. He could handle it for a few months, but if the payout didn't rise, he'd end up losing his own company. Or at the very least, have to take on a partner, and that would feel like losing it. He understood even more how Jasmine felt when Dean sold off a part of Kennedy Holdings.

Matt had told him about his first meeting. He'd disliked most of the board members, especially Dean Kennedy. He'd happened to meet Jasmine and immediately liked her, but who wouldn't? Apparently, some of the board members. He hoped, going forward, Matt would be able to sway the members to do what was good for the company.

He picked up the phone and dialed.

"Hello," Matt answered.

Nick leaned back in his chair, his eyes not leaving the check. "Hey, Matt. How are you?"

"Hi, Nick. I'm good. I was going to call you. I have an appointment next week, and the client wants to meet you."

"Local?" He hoped so. He didn't want to be far from Jasmine.

"Couple hours drive. On Wednesday."

"Okay. Email me a reminder. The reason I called was to ask you to send me the financials from Kennedy Holdings." He tapped the check.

"They didn't give me one. I would have sent it to you."

"They should have," Nick snapped. "I need you to call them. Get the copy, and request you get one every month."

"Sure. I'll do it as soon as we hang up. Is there a problem?"

Nick rubbed the back of his neck. He shouldn't take out his frustration on Matt. "Sorry. I think something's wrong with the numbers." A thought entered his head, and he couldn't force it away. "Can you also call Jasmine? Ask her to send you the financials. Try not to sound suspicious. Maybe say she was the friendliest face."

"So, you want financials from both sources to compare?"

"Exactly. I want them both to be the same, but I'm not counting on it."

~~~

Jasmine bustled around the dining room, rearranging the three place settings Lydia had already set up, and depositing a pitcher of ice water near the center of the table. Back in the kitchen, she surveyed the serving utensils and trivets, then took them to the table.

She slid her hands down the sides of her baby belly and pants as she glanced at the clock. Nick would arrive any moment, and Josh would come down then. She peeked in the oven at the perfectly browned Cornish game hens. The delicious aroma made her stomach growl. Lydia had prepared the meal before leaving for the day and placed everything in the oven to stay warm.

The doorbell rang, and she rushed to answer it. "Nick!" She threw her arms around his neck and kissed him. She'd seen him a couple of times since he gave her the ring, but tonight, the three of them would discuss wedding plans.

She grabbed his hand and dragged him into the house as Josh hastened down the stairs. "Come into the dining room. Josh, why don't you get drinks while I serve the food?"

Nick held on when she tried to extract her hand. "I'll help you bring out the food."

She led him to the kitchen, but he stopped beside the stove.

He wrapped his arms around her. "And I get to do this once more." He kissed her. "I missed you."

"But it's been only two days."

He kissed the tip of her nose. "Too long. I'm looking forward to coming home to you every night."

She grinned. "Me, too. But I'm hungry." She pulled out of his arms and snatched up oven mitts from the counter, then opened the oven.

The three golden brown Cornish hens sat on individual plates and smelled delicious. Jasmine plucked a knife from a magnetic rack and set it in front of the hens. "Can you cut them all in half lengthwise?"

He picked up the knife. "Sure."

Jasmine lifted out bowls of mashed potatoes, gravy, and broccoli and placed them on another tray, then removed their lids. She added a warm basket of napkin covered biscuits.

Nick picked up the basket and handed it to her then carried the tray to the dining room.

She followed behind. "I could have carried that."

"I'm here, so you didn't have to." He unloaded the dishes onto the table.

They returned to the kitchen, and Nick finished cutting

the hens then picked up two of the plates, and she grabbed the third. Once the plates were placed at their settings, Nick helped her into her seat and sat beside her with Josh across the table.

Jasmine loaded her plate with way too much food. The baby made her ravenous, but he must be squashing her stomach because she never ate as much as she thought she should. She'd started to have several snacks a day and hoped they'd be easy to cut out once he was born.

Nick rubbed her leg. "Should we have the wedding in a month?"

A quick dose of panic ran through her. "That soon?"

"I want a small wedding. I'm pretty sure you do as well." He rubbed her tummy. "I want to be married before this little guy is born."

She wrapped her hand around his. "Are you getting all traditional on me?"

He chuckled. "Traditional would be marrying you *before* you were pregnant. So, what do you say? A wedding in a month in Rochester?"

Josh cleared his throat. "You know, Jasmine's going to be eight months pregnant in a month. Do you really want to take the chance she'll go into labor from flying?"

Nick's eyes widened. "That can happen?"

"Yes. It happened to the wife of a friend of mine. Six weeks early. Fortunately, it was after their return flight, so they got to be home while the baby stayed in the hospital."

"Okay. We'll have the wedding here. I'll fly my family in."

Jasmine set her glass down. "We can have the wedding in the living room. Your family can stay here. There's plenty of room."

"Thank you. What about a preacher or justice of the peace?"

"What about Judge Silver?" Josh asked.

"You could get a judge to come to the house?" Nick asked.

Jasmine beamed. It would bring her father closer. "Yes. He was Dad's best friend. He'd probably enjoy officiating for his old friend's daughter. We could have the wedding September 26 or 27, whichever day he's free."

Josh tapped his phone. "I'll call him tomorrow."

Jasmine plucked her phone from a pocket, and typed *Guests* on a fresh note. "Who do we invite? I want Rhonda, Anna and Holly." She added their names on her list as well as Nick's family. "What about Uncle Dean?"

"No!"

She frowned at the two men. That was unanimous. "Why not?"

Josh slammed his fork down. "Do you need to ask? Look what he did to us. I can't even walk into my own company."

Jasmine bit her lip. She shouldn't have mentioned him. "Okay. No Uncle Dean. What about Aunt Pam and our cousins?" She hadn't seen them in a couple years.

"Sure, you can ask them. I don't know if they'll come. Maybe if you tell them Uncle Dean won't be there."

"Okay." She wrote them down and glanced at Nick. "You want Alex there?"

"Yes, and…Let me think about it."

She was pretty sure he'd been about to say a name, and at the last moment, changed his mind. Was it someone he thought wouldn't fit in, or someone he didn't want her to talk to? It wasn't something she wanted to dwell on right now. "With so few people, I think Lydia can handle the meals. I'll discuss it with her. What else?"

Nick squeezed her hand. "Your wedding dress."

Her heart did a slow flip. "I'd always wanted to wear my mother's dress." She stared down at her increasing size. "But it won't fit." There was no way she'd tear apart her mother's dress to resize it, making it nothing like the dress in her parents' wedding pictures.

Nick squeezed her hand. "I'm sorry. I'm sure you'll find the perfect dress."

She drew in a deep breath. "I'll ask Anna and Holly to shop with me this coming week."

"How about a photographer?" Josh asked.

She patted her tummy. "I really don't want to memorialize me in a wedding dress."

Josh typed on his phone. "I'll make a couple calls. I'm sure we can find someone who can take tasteful pregnant bride pictures."

"Flowers! And a cake." Jasmine typed on her phone. "I'll call about those on Monday."

"Honeymoon," Nick said.

Her cheeks warmed. At seven months pregnant, she shouldn't be flustered by that word. "We can't fly anywhere."

He stared into her eyes and ran a knuckle down her cheek. "I'll think of something."

Her heart swelled. "I love you."

Josh cleared his throat. "Um. Okay. I think we're done." He picked up his dishes and left the room.

Jasmine giggled. "I think you chased him off."

"Good. Now what would you like to do?"

"Watch a movie?" She wanted to snuggle with Nick.

"I brought my overnight bag."

Her eyes widened. "Here?" She hadn't seen it.

He grinned and rubbed her tummy. "I think Josh knows what we do when we're alone."

"But here? And where's your bag?"

He pointed over his shoulder. "It's on the porch." He stood and helped her to her feet, wrapping his arms around her, at least most of the way around. "I don't think Josh will mind if I stay over."

"Okay. A movie, and, um, bed." At least Josh's room wasn't next to hers any more. When he returned home after college, he'd moved all his belongings to a suite on the third floor.

Nick leaned over her tummy and kissed her. "Okay. I'll get my bag."

Other than the distressing news about her father, and that guest Nick held back, her life was perfect.

Chapter 15

Nick clapped a hand to Matt's shoulder as they followed the hostess to their table. "Sorry to make you shuffle your schedule."

"Not a problem. My boss is pretty agreeable about stuff like that." He grinned.

"Yeah, well. I hope your boss doesn't overwork you to the point you want to leave."

"I'm getting paid pretty generously for the Kennedy Holdings gig. Closing in on that boat I want."

The hostess escorted them to a table then handed them menus. "I'll send your server shortly."

Nick set his menu down. "Tell me your strategy for Arlington Dynamics. I tried talking to them last year and got nowhere."

Matt leaned in. "I studied your notes and everything I could get on them. They tried someone else and it didn't work out, so I'm highlighting our differences." He continued to describe his presentation, with an interruption from the server to give their selections.

Nick kept the conversation light over the meal, and dove into the most important part of their lunch during dessert. "Did you get both financials for Kennedy Holdings?"

Matt pulled some papers from an inside jacket pocket. "Yes. I started comparing them, and you're right." He spread two pages side-by-side on the table. "Everything checked out except these numbers." He pointed to several yellow highlighted numbers on each page.

Whoever had doctored the statement—probably Dean—had made it appear Kennedy Holdings' income was much lower, which affected Nick's payout. If he'd gotten the amount he should have, it would have more than covered his loan payment. Dean had probably stolen the difference.

A voice near the door caught his attention. He'd always notice Jasmine—who shouldn't be here! She'd said she was having lunch with her brother, but he hadn't expected her to show up at the same restaurant as him. He turned his head, hoping she wouldn't see him.

"Nick!" She hurried across the restaurant with Josh trailing behind. Timing couldn't have been worse.

Matt dropped his napkin over the papers.

Jasmine's gaze bounced between him and Matt. "I wasn't aware you two knew each other."

This wasn't the time to go into long explanations. He needed to convince her nothing was going on, and explain to her later about the company. Something he should have told her before now. "I—"

Matt grinned. Easy for him. "I'm one of Nick's clients."

"And I'm his fiancée. Nick, Matt's our new board member. Quite a coincidence."

Nick stood and took her hand. "Jasmine, I've got to get back to business. I'll see you tonight."

She nodded. "All right." She eyed Matt. "It was nice seeing you again." Her gaze dropped to the table with the word 'Kennedy' peeking from the napkin.

She snatched up one sheet and shook it at Matt. "What is this? I gave you confidential information, and you're sharing it with someone else?"

Matt glanced at Nick, then back to Jasmine. "I, uh,

thought he could tell me about some of the tech companies you're invested in."

She planted a hand on her hip. "They're our companies. You should have come to me."

"Sorry."

She stared wide-eyed at Nick, maybe seeing guilt on his face. "He's not the one who owns ten percent. It's you."

Nick's heart plummeted at the accusation in her voice. She'd found out in the worst possible way. "Jasmine, I need to explain this to you."

"No need to explain. I was just a means to an end."

"That's not true." He took her hand. "I love you. I did this for you."

She yanked her hand away. "That's not how it looks to me." Her eyes swam in tears.

"That's ridiculous."

"So, now I'm ridiculous!"

He'd made it worse. Her emotion swings worked against him. "You're not ridiculous. You're the woman I'd do anything for."

She bit her lip. "I can't believe you did this to me. You know how the sale affected me and you said nothing. Every time I mentioned it, and you said nothing, made it a lie." She pulled off her engagement ring and slapped it on the table. "I don't want to see you again." A tear trickled down her cheek, then she stalked away from him.

"Jasmine!" His world crumbled. He had to convince her he'd done it for her.

Matt grabbed his arm. "She's not going to listen to you right now. Give her a chance to calm down."

Nick didn't think he should wait, but he sunk into his chair, and ran his hands through his hair. "I can't lose her."

"In a couple days, she should be able to see reason."

Nick clenched his fists. "A couple days? I don't think I

can go a couple hours." Jasmine had to talk to him again. She needed a chance to think about it. Maybe she thought he'd approached Dean with some information he'd gleaned from her, and hadn't known about the bidding war. If he'd told her already, she might have been upset, but nothing like this. The betrayal in her eyes would haunt him, and it wouldn't be fixed until they talked. He had to beg her forgiveness.

Josh stopped at the table and glared. "You should have told her."

Nick grimaced. "I intended to, but it never seemed like the right time. Jasmine's so emotional, I was afraid she'd take it wrong."

Josh leaned in. "Finding out you kept it a secret from her, she took it really the wrong way."

Nick rubbed the back of his neck. "Yeah. I've got to fix this somehow."

Josh straightened. "I hope you can. By the way, thanks for buying the ten percent. Hopefully, Kennedy Holdings will be totally family owned again."

"I hope so." The only way that would happen was if Jasmine still married him. He didn't see that happening at the moment.

Josh glanced over his shoulder. "I've got to go talk to her. Give her a day or so before you try to explain."

Nick's almost brother-in-law walked away. At least Josh understood the reason Nick bought into the company.

~~~

Jasmine stepped onto the sidewalk and backed up to the building. She heaved in, trying not to let the tears that blurred her vision fall. Somehow, she'd get through this. She rubbed her protruding belly. Originally, her plan had been to raise this baby alone. She's go back to that, but it would be harder now.

She'd envisioned two loving parents for her baby, and now she was alone again. Her baby's daddy had a face now. A lying face. One she didn't want to see again, but he'd want to be part of his son's life.

Josh stepped through the doors and glanced from side to side. He joined her and gave her a hug. "You have to think about why Nick would do this."

"I don't want to talk about it." She twisted away and marched down the sidewalk.

He fell in beside her. "Jasmine—"

She flung her index finger up. "If you're going to talk, you can leave me now."

"Fine."

Maybe Nick had planned this from the beginning. He could have followed her from the funeral service to the bar, waited until she was half drunk before approaching her. It must have been a shock for him that she'd left while he was in the bathroom, and then she couldn't remember him and he had to start all over again.

But that didn't make sense.

Josh grabbed her arm and steered her to the curb. "Here's my car."

"Oh, yeah." He held the door open. She got in, and buckled her seatbelt.

Nick had told her he only found out who she was after seeing her on a news report about Uncle Dean's takeover. If that was the case, it made sense that she met him about two weeks later. That part didn't seem to be a lie.

Josh started the car. "Do you want me to drop you back at work, or do you want to go home?"

She couldn't imagine getting anything done the rest of the day. "Take me home. I'll call Rhonda." She made the call, telling Rhonda she wasn't coming back in for the afternoon.

Jasmine thought back to the charity event. That's where she met Nick, but not really. He'd lied by not telling her they'd met before, been together intimately. He'd only told her the truth after he found out she was pregnant. He had to stake his claim on the baby. If not for that, would he have ever told her about that night?

The car engine turned off, and Jasmine opened her eyes. Her whole family now sat in the car with her. Josh and the little one growing inside her. And she was alone. Her world had tumbled to ruin in an instant. And once again, she'd have to rebuild.

She'd taken so long to get out, Josh rounded the car and opened her door. He squatted beside her. "Are you all right?"

One look at his face led to more tears. "No." Stupid pregnancy hormones. Although, that wasn't all it was this time. Except, maybe the hormones were making it seem worse than it was. Her brain was a swirling stew of pain, secrets, betrayal…and love.

"Do you want to talk about it?"

"No. I can't."

He took her hand and stood. "You know I'm here for you."

She let him help her from the car. "I know."

She wrapped her arms around him, and he held her close as she drew on his love. With Josh's help she'd make it through, just like after their father died and when Uncle Dean took over Kennedy Holdings.

He patted her back. "Come on. Let's go in." He led her up the steps and inside. "Do you want something to eat?"

She shook her head. "I'm not hungry. Maybe later."

"All right. Why don't you go lie down?"

Her energy sapped, she trudged up the stairs but wasn't likely to sleep. Her heart ached. If not for her son, she might think she could die from a broken heart.

~~~

Jasmine leaned back in her chair at the quiet office. She couldn't go home yet, even though Holly had tried to convince her to not stay late. It was Friday and everyone had cleared out already, leaving her alone without their pity. For the past week, whenever her mind had time to wander, it always turned to Nick. All the fun things they'd done, talking together, how wonderful it was to be in his bed. Her heart bled with every remembrance.

Maybe she should talk to him. She'd rejected all his calls, and there had been a lot of them. But she wasn't sure if she could face him. It'd be too easy to believe everything he said, but would it be true?

She grabbed a fresh bottle of mineral water from the top of her filing cabinet and headed to the kitchen at the end of the hall. From the refrigerator, she pulled out a plastic lemon with a big, black J on it. She cracked open her bottle and squeezed the juice into it, and returned the lemon to its place. After capping and swirling the bottle, she re-opened it and took a swig. Uh. A whole body shiver shook her at the bitter taste. She poured a quarter of the bottle out and filled it from the water dispenser, then took a taste. Not perfect, but better. She headed back to her office.

Jasmine sank into her chair with a sigh and leaned back. She'd always been comfortable in Kennedy Holdings, visiting the offices from the time she was a small child. After Mrs. Wilson retired, her father had her office repainted and furnished, and presented it to Jasmine with a big red bow on the door. He'd been as excited as her that day. It was so much nicer than the desk in a cubicle she'd had before.

It was getting easier to think of the good times with her

father. Much better than thinking about—not going there again.

The work in front of her still wasn't getting done. She sighed and gulped down more water, renewing her effort.

A short time later, her door opened, making her jump and her heart pound. "Uncle Dean! What are you doing here?" Most days, he left shortly after five.

He glanced at her desk before returning his gaze to hers. "Just thought I'd check on you." He stepped into the room and sat in the chair across from her.

He'd never come to her office before. If he needed to see her, he'd call and have her come to him. They hadn't had a personal conversation since her father died, and she and Josh hadn't had him to the house since, either.

She frowned. Even when they'd been friendlier, he'd never shown concern about her. "I'm okay."

His eyes flicked to the half finished water bottle on her desk and back to her. "Are you, my dear?"

There was something creepy about that, but she couldn't make sense of it. For the first time ever, her uncle scared her.

"Yes, of course."

He gave her a smarmy smile. "Not despondent because your fiancé dumped you?"

"I-he…" Her uncle didn't need the details. She wasn't surprised it had gotten back to him that she no longer wore Nick's ring. The office buzz stopped when she walked into a room. She grabbed her water and took a few swallows, giving her time to pull herself together. "I'm not discussing that."

His gaze followed the bottle back to the desk. "I'm really sorry it has to end this way. I always liked you the best."

A chill furrowed up her spine. "End? You're firing me? You can't do that!" She stood, and a wave of dizziness made her catch her breath as she grabbed for the desk.

Dean got to his feet and leaned a hip against her desk,

shaking his head. "I'm sorry, dear. That's not enough. You're committing suicide." He said it matter-of-fact, as if reading data from a report.

"What!" She rubbed her forehead. Her thoughts were muddled. "I wouldn't do that." She dropped back into her chair.

He shook her water bottle. "You already have."

"No!" Her gaze veered from his face, to the bottle and back. He'd poisoned her. Tears tracked down her cheeks. The baby would die with her, and Nick would lose them both. He'd been so excited about becoming a father.

"First you lost your father, and then the father of your child leaves you. Everyone's seen how despondent you've been."

Her brain slowed as she fit the words together. "Why are you doing this?"

He leaned over her. "I spent forty years at Arthur's side, and he treated me like any other employee. Sure, he paid well, but I deserve a piece of this company. He was ready to push me aside for you and Josh. With you two out of the way, I'll have it all."

She blinked up at the man she thought she'd known, but hadn't since her father died.

He pulled a memory key out of his pocket. "I've got the perfect good-bye letter ready to put on your computer."

Jasmine couldn't hold her eyes open. Would everybody believe she'd taken her own life?

Chapter 16

Nick had been miserable the past week. Worse than before, when he and Jasmine had only shared one night. And now there was the baby to think of. He couldn't lose the woman he loved and their child.

He had to make another effort to talk to Jasmine. He'd gone by the house, but Josh had told him she'd been working a lot of late nights. Maybe in her own territory, she'd be comfortable enough to talk to him.

He parked in the nearly empty lot next to the Kennedy building, picked up the bouquet of flowers, and hurried to the door. He yanked the handle, only to find the door locked. A security guard sat at a desk against the far wall, and Nick knocked on the glass.

The man's head popped up from whatever he was viewing. His voice came over a nearby speaker. "Can I help you?"

Nick stared straight at the man. "I'm here to see Jasmine Kennedy."

"She didn't call down that anyone was coming."

"It's a surprise." He held up the bouquet of daisies, Jasmine's favorite.

The guard stood. "Let me see ID." He took his time getting to the door, and Nick plastered his license to the glass. The man leaned in and nodded, then turned away, returning to the desk.

Nick hoped his name hadn't been removed from the approved list. A minute passed before the man surveyed him again. "Come on in."

Nick blew out a long breath as the door buzzed, and opened it. He strode through and to the elevator. "Thanks." At the last second, he decided to take the stairs and hurried past the two elevators. He needed to expend some nervous energy before talking to Jasmine.

He stepped onto the second floor, and caught the door so it closed without a sound. Quiet and emptiness surrounded him as if no one was on the floor. It seemed like Jasmine would be nervous all alone in the huge building, but she'd probably been in these offices from the time she was a young child.

He was halfway to her door when voices made him pause. He crept closer.

"I'm sorry, dear. That's not enough. You're committing suicide." The voice was familiar.

The blood froze in Nick's veins. The past week was nothing like the pain roaring through him now.

"What! I wouldn't do that." A chair squeaked.

Water sloshed. "You already have." Jasmine's uncle.

"No!" The sorrow in her voice tore at him.

"First you lost your father, and then the father of your child leaves you. Everyone's seen how despondent you've been."

"Why are you doing this?" Her words were slurred.

Nick stopped, dropped the flowers and whipped out his phone, setting it to silent mode. He texted Josh, half listening to the man he now despised. *Jasmine poisoned. Get emts to her office.* He hit send, with the hope Josh would see it immediately then sprinted for her door.

Dean raged. "I spent forty years at Arthur's side, and he

treated me like any other employee. Sure, he paid well, but I deserve a piece of this company. He was ready to push me aside for you and Josh. With you two out of the way, I'll have it all. I've got the perfect good-bye letter ready to put on your computer."

Nick reached the door and with a roar raced into the office. Dean stood across the desk from a slumped Jasmine.

Dean swung around, a water bottle in his hand, and the smirk dropped from his lips. "Who the hell are you?"

"Justice." He punched Dean in the jaw, and the man dropped.

Pain exploded in his hand, but he didn't care. All that mattered was saving Jasmine. He framed her head in his hands. Her unfocused eyes stared at him. Her cheeks were flushed and her forehead beaded in sweat. He hoped he wasn't too late. "Jasmine, talk to me."

"I'm sorry."

He didn't want those to be the last words she said, especially since he was the one who was sorry. "Was the poison in the water bottle?"

Tears streaming down her face. "Yes."

He bent her to the side and shoved a finger into the back of her throat. She gagged and warm water spewed across his hand, splattering to the floor. He should have grabbed the waste basket, but he didn't care. Jasmine was more important. After she stopped gagging, he pressed his finger into her mouth again, wanting to make sure her stomach was empty. More of the poisonous fluid left her.

Nick pushed her against the chair back, snatched up a tissue from the desk and wiped her mouth. Her head swayed to the side.

He picked up her desk phone, hit the button for an outside line and dialed 9-1-1.

"9-1-1. What's your emergency?"

"My fiancée's been poisoned. I need paramedics and the police."

"We've already had a call for your location. They should be there in less than five minutes."

Thank God Josh saw the text. "Good."

He dropped the phone in its cradle. Jasmine might die before help arrived. Maybe he should make her drink water. It might slow down the poison entering her system. He raced to the hall and swung his head in both directions. There was a break room somewhere on the floor. End of the hall. He turned right and ran like death nipped at his heels.

He skidded to a stop inside the room and did a quick inspection. Water dispenser in the corner. Plastic cups sat on top. He grabbed one and an interminable time later the glass was full. He picked up another and filled it, too, then ran back to Jasmine's office, one in each hand.

Her head was turned to the side, eyes closed.

"No! No! Honey, wake up!"

Her eyes half opened. She whispered one word. "Nick?"

He set one glass on the desk and held the other to her lips. "Jasmine, you have to drink this. Please. I don't know what else to do." Her face blurred, and he blinked a few times to clear his vision.

She opened her mouth and swallowed a small amount.

"Good. Good. Take more. As much as you can."

She took more small swallows. He wished he could dump both glasses down her throat and get it all into her at once.

In the silence of the office, the elevator dinged from down the hall. He hoped that was the paramedics. He raced out the door, and the sight of blue uniforms and a stretcher sent relief washing over him.

"Here! Down here. Quick!"

Two men guided the wheeled bed with two boxes on top

toward him and entered the office. One rushed to Jasmine and the other to Dean.

"Forget about him! He tried to kill her," he motioned to Jasmine, "and I knocked him out. Restrain him if you've got a pair of cuffs on you."

The shorter paramedic said, "Sorry, sir. We have to treat him, too."

Nick picked the water bottle up from the floor, and held it out to the other rescuer. "He put poison in her water."

"Do you know what it is?"

He shook his head. "No idea. But I made her throw up and started giving her water."

The man unscrewed the cap and took a whiff then wrinkled his nose. "It might be meth." He set the recapped bottle on the desk.

The shorter paramedic bent over Dean while this one plucked a penlight from his pocket and flashed a light into Jasmine's eyes. "Eyes react, but they're slow." He took her wrist and looked at his watch. "It's fast but weak."

"She's pregnant." If Jasmine survived...Not if. She would survive. What about their baby? What harm was this poison doing?

"How far along?"

"Seven-and-a-half months."

"Any allergies?"

Nick shrugged. "None that I know of." He hoped that wouldn't cause her harm.

The rescuer entered data on a tablet and pulled a bag of clear liquid from the box. He glanced at his partner. "Ready, Alex?"

Alex stood. "Yeah. This guy's fine."

Together, the men lifted Jasmine and gently laid her on the stretcher. Alex attached the bag to a pole while the taller Paramedic slipped a needle into the back of her hand and taped it into place. He opened the valve and the liquid dripped. Then he poured a small amount of water from the poisoned bottle into a vial and labeled it, leaving the bottle on the desk. "We're ready to roll. You can meet us at the hospital."

Nick glanced between Jasmine and Dean. He wanted to follow the ambulance to the hospital, but he also needed to make sure to tell the police the whole story of Dean's treachery.

The sympathetic man squeezed Nick's shoulder. "You won't be able to see her right away, anyway. I'm sure the police won't be long." The elevator dinged. "I bet that's them."

Alex stepped into the hall. "Hold the elevator. Got an emergency coming down."

Nick hurried to the stretcher before it left the room. "Wait!" He held Jasmine's face between his hands. Her eyes didn't open, and it tore another hole in his heart. He touched his lips to hers. "Jasmine, don't let go. Hold on for the baby. For us."

He stepped back, and took a deep breath. She needed to get to the hospital ASAP.

Nick's strength left him. He dropped into the chair in front of the desk, and closed his eyes. He'd held it together for Jasmine, but her life was now in medical hands.

"Sir, we need to ask some questions. We got a report of a possible poisoning."

Nick snapped back to attention. A police officer stood beside the desk, a notebook in his hand, while a second officer used a gloved hand to tuck the water bottle into a Ziploc bag and labeled it. The paramedic must have told them about the bottle.

Nick pointed at Dean. "Jasmine's uncle poisoned her and likely killed her father."

The officer leaned back against the desk. "I'm officer Grice, and he's Officer Ellis. Tell us what happened tonight."

Chapter 17

Nick raced past cars in the parking garage, and barreled through the doors of the emergency room, then hurried to the desk. "Jasmine Kennedy was brought in by ambulance. I'm her fiancé."

The nurse tapped at her keyboard. "Your name?"

"Nick Lawson."

"Miss Kennedy's brother said you'd be coming." She pointed to a corridor. "Take the elevator to the fifth floor, then turn right into the family waiting room."

Nick ran to the elevators and pushed the up button. He rocked on one foot, then the other. The cars were on upper floors, and taking too long. While he waited on elevators, Jasmine fought for her life. "Come on. Get down here."

He stepped back and scanned the area. Stairs on the left. He rushed to them, banged the door open and took the steps two at a time, then shoved through the door labeled *Five*. He stepped into the family waiting room and hurried to Josh.

He sat, elbows on knees, chin on his folded hands.

"Have you heard anything?" Nick asked.

Josh's head snapped up, and he straightened. "Not yet. But that's probably good, right?"

Yeah. Good. It had to be.

Josh looked as bad as Nick felt. His red-rimmed eyes were glassy, his usually perfect hair was messed up from fingers running through it. The stress in his face made him appear ten years older. "At least she's got a chance. If you hadn't gone to talk to her, she would have been..." He bowed his head and covered his eyes, taking long ragged breaths.

Nick sat down beside Josh and put his arm over the man's stiff shoulders. "She's going to pull through. I know she is."

Nick sat back in his chair, and leaned his head against the wall, staring at the drop ceiling, as Josh slowly recovered.

This shouldn't have happened. If the police had questioned Dean before now about his brother's death, he wouldn't have taken a chance on killing Jasmine.

Now, Jasmine fought for her life and their baby's. He thanked God that he chose that night to talk to her.

She was a fighter. She wouldn't give up. He hoped their son was a fighter, too. If he could exchange his life for theirs, he'd do it in an instant.

A shoe scuffed the floor then a male voice spoke. "Family of Jasmine Kennedy?"

Nick jackknifed to his feet. Josh was just as quick as they hurried to the doctor standing at the waiting room doorway.

"How is she?" Nick and Josh said together.

"She's holding her own. Her blood pressure was low when they brought her in, but we've stabilized it. Then her temperature spiked, so we've got her packed in ice. We couldn't give her medication to lower the temperature because there's already a risk of placenta separation due to the methamphetamine."

Josh stiffened. "What? That bastard gave her meth?"

The doctor nodded. "That's what was in the water bottle and the symptoms match."

At least she was still alive. "What about the baby?"

"We're monitoring. So far, so good. If we see any signs

of fetal distress, we'll have to do a c-section."

Nick's gut clenched. "But the baby's not due for six more weeks."

"Waiting may not be an option. In the morning, we'll do an ultrasound to check the condition of the placenta."

"Can we see her?" Josh asked.

"In about ten minutes, and then one at a time. A nurse will come get you." He hurried down the corridor.

Nick sank into the nearest chair, his fear somewhat eased. She'd survived the worst of it.

Josh sat a few chairs over. "Thank God. Jasmine doesn't deserve this."

Nick stared down the hallway. He'd come close to losing Jasmine, and it shredded his heart. He needed to be with her. He couldn't imagine how hard this would be if she had to face it alone.

A nurse stepped into the room. "Family of Jasmine Kennedy."

Both men stood.

"One of you can see her now. You've got fifteen minutes and then the other can go in."

"Josh, you go first, then go home. I want to see if I can stay with her." If they didn't let him stay the night, maybe he'd at least get to stay longer than fifteen minutes.

Josh squeezed Nick's shoulder. "Thanks." He followed the woman to Jasmine.

Nick couldn't sit. He paced, his thoughts never wavering from how much he'd show Jasmine he loved her. He stared out the window. At two in the morning, there were few cars on the street. He strode to the water dispenser near the door, filled a cup and gulped it down, then crushed the cup and dropped it into the trash. He spun around and marched across the room then back again.

Josh strode down the hall and stopped in front of Nick.

"Your turn. She's too pale. I don't know how all that beeping hasn't awakened her. She's in room five-thirty-six."

Nick sucked in a breath, preparing himself for what he'd see. "I'll talk to you tomorrow." He took measured steps down the corridor, checking the room numbers, wanting to see her, but afraid he'd break down when he saw her. He rubbed his sweaty palms on his pant legs. He didn't want Jasmine to look as deathly as he'd last seen her, but had to be ready for anything. He pulled in a long breath.

The door stood open, a curtain hiding the head of the bed. Jasmine's lower body and the swell of their baby drew him in. The galloping rate of his son's heartbeat reassured him they were both alive. He stepped to the far side of the bed, and kissed Jasmine's forehead. It was warmer than usual, but she was no longer packed in ice. Her color was better than when the paramedics had whisked her away. He wanted to run his fingers through her soft hair, but was afraid he'd dislodge the oxygen tube under her nose.

He took the hand that was clear of tubes. "Jasmine, I love you. Please keep strong. You have a lot to live for."

Her hand twitched. He'd take it as a good sign.

He ran a finger down the side of her face. He hadn't seen her in over a week, and missed her, but more than that, he'd been heartbroken. He'd accomplished nothing work-wise, no matter how hard he'd tried.

He'd imagined visits to see his son and yearning to hold Jasmine, but only seeing hostility in her eyes. He needed to fix this. She was hurting, too. He'd caused her pain by trying to protect her the wrong way. He hoped he'd get the chance to tell her everything.

The curtain rings scraped across metal. "Sorry, sir. It's time to leave."

"But I need to be with her. I need to be here when she wakes up."

Pity swept the nurse's face. "Struggling against the drug exhausted her. She'll likely sleep all night."

He stood, resigned. "All right." He planted a soft kiss on Jasmine's forehead. "Keep fighting, honey. I'll be back in the morning."

At the door, he turned for another glimpse. The only sign she still breathed was the monitor displaying her respiration. He dropped his eyes to her belly. There were so many ways everything could still fall apart.

~~~

"Morning!"

Nick opened his eyes, and stared up at Matt. He'd crashed on the couch at his office since it was closer to the hospital than his apartment. He sat up and rubbed his face, not expecting to actually sleep. "What time is it?"

"Six-forty."

Nick squinted at him. "Do you always come in this early?"

"It beats traffic, but no. I wanted to run through the report one last time before the board meeting."

Nick stood and stretched. "There probably won't be a board meeting today."

Matt grinned. "You talking about the fact Dean Kennedy was arrested?"

Nick raised his eyebrows. "You heard about that?"

"It was on the radio this morning. Attempted murder. Who'd he try to kill?"

"Jasmine. She's in the hospital."

Matt grabbed his arm. "What? What happened? She's okay, isn't she? "

"She's alive." At least, he hoped she still was since he hadn't gotten a call otherwise. "He put meth in her water bottle. Fortunately, I arrived in time and found them."

"God. How about the baby?"

Nick ran a hand through his hair. "As of last night, he's holding his own. I have to get back to the hospital."

Matt slapped a hand on his shoulder. "Good luck, man."

On the elevator ride down, Nick decided to walk the six blocks to the hospital. Considering traffic, it would probably be faster. He hurried into the hospital lobby and detoured into the gift shop. He picked out a short vase of flowers that included a few daisies. Then rode the elevator to the fifth floor. He headed straight to the nurses' station when the doors opened and hovered beside the desk while the nurse finished writing notes.

"I'm checking on Jasmine Kennedy."

"Are you family?"

"I'm her fiancé. I'm on your list."

She frowned. "Let me check her chart." She tapped on her computer and scanned the screen. "What's your name?"

"Nick Lawson."

She looked up at him. "Yes, you're on the list."

"So, how is she?"

She studied the chart again. "It was a quiet night. She's scheduled for an ultrasound at nine-thirty."

No emergencies was positive. "Has she been awake?"

She checked her chart again. "The nurse on duty spoke to her at five o'clock."

Wonderful. "Can I see her?"

"We don't normally allow visitors until after nine, but since you're nearly family, you can go down."

"Is she still in five-thirty-six?"

"Yes."

The door to her room stood open, but the curtain was drawn across farther than before. He paused. The heart monitor beeped the quick pace of the baby. Jasmine must be out of danger since hers was silent. He took a deep breath and stepped into sight. Her eyes were closed, but this time she appeared to be sleeping. He couldn't resist touching her. He set the flowers on the rolling table beside her bed and kissed her forehead. He took her hand then sat on the chair beside her. "Good morning, honey."

Her eyes flickered, but didn't open. "Nick?" Her voice was not just soft, but weak.

"I'm here. I'm so glad you're awake."

Her eyes opened, and when she tugged her hand from his, his heart squeezed in pain. But then she placed her palm against his cheek, and his heart soared.

Her little finger touched his ear. "I'm sorry I got so mad at you. I know you could have bought a part of Kennedy Holdings without knowing me."

"Honey, I bought the ten percent so you wouldn't lose it. A client of Alex's told him it was for sale. Two other companies bid against me. Once we were married, the company would be whole again."

Tears streaked her cheeks. "Oh, Nick." She slipped her hand to the back of his neck, and he leaned forward to kiss her properly.

She forgave him. It felt nearly as wonderful as knowing she survived.

She scanned the room. "Do you know why I'm in the hospital?"

He frowned. "You don't remember?"

"It's kind of fuzzy. I'm not sure what's real." She bit her lip.

"Your uncle put methamphetamine in your bottle of water."

She shook her head. "That can't be. I cracked the seal myself." Her eyes widened. "My lemon. I have one of those plastic lemons in the break room refrigerator. He must have added it to that." She squeezed his hand. "It's still there. I don't want someone else to use it."

"I'll call the cop I talked to."

"Tell him it has a big, black J on it."

He stepped away from the bed and took out his phone, calling the number on the card the officer had given him the night before.

He relayed the lemon information and was assured it would be taken care of right away. That would be more evidence against Dean. Hopefully, they'd find his fingerprints.

He put his phone away. "What else do you remember?"

"Uncle Dean visited me in my office. I'm not sure if that's real. He's never done it before."

Nick wanted to punch Dean all over again. "It was real. He came to gloat and watch you die. He had a suicide note ready to put on your computer."

Her eyes widened, and she covered her mouth. "I remember that. Then you rushed in and saved me."

She lifted her arm and he leaned in to hug her. She gasped and scrunched over.

He leaned away. "What's wrong?" His gut twisted at the pain in her eyes.

She grabbed her belly. "I think something tore. It hurts."

He pushed the call button over and over.

Jasmine panted, her breath coming in short bursts.

He hit the button again, but couldn't wait any longer. He took three quick steps and collided with the nurse as she rounded the curtain. They steadied each other, then she asked, "What's wrong?"

"She felt something pull, and now she's in pain."

The nurse checked the monitor. "The baby's heartbeat is still strong and steady. Show me where."

Jasmine rubbed her hand over the spot on the side of her

belly she hadn't stopped touching. "Right here."

The nurse gave a quick nod. "I'll page the doctor." She hurried from the room.

Jasmine eased back against the pillow and rubbed her belly. "It still hurts, but it's not as sharp."

Nick held her hand and rubbed her shoulders. The tension tightening her body couldn't be good for her or the baby.

A long five minutes later, the doctor walked in. "I hear you're having pain."

"Yes. It was sharp at first, and now it throbs."

"Show me where."

Jasmine placed her hands in the same spot she'd been rubbing. "Here."

The doctor gently probed. "I'm moving up your ultrasound. I tried to get the portable one, but it's not available, so we'll have to take you to the diagnostic floor. You'll have to stay in the bed, because I don't want to move you."

He checked the fetal monitor. "I'll be back in a few minutes."

Jasmine gripped Nick's hand. "What do you think is wrong?"

He pushed back her hair. "Let's wait for the ultrasound." He sure hoped this was nothing. The words from the doctor the night before echoed through his head. *Separation of the placenta.* Their baby had to be okay.

"I know this isn't normal." Tears shimmered in her eyes.

He wished he could take her pain away. He skimmed his fingers along her jaw. "Honey, we're in the hospital. If something's wrong, we're right where we need to be. Try to relax."

She dropped her head to the pillow and took deep breaths.

Nick sent a text to Josh. *Jasmine awake. Had sharp pain. Waiting for ultrasound.*

The room filled with a flurry of activity led by the doctor. Two orderlies positioned themselves on each end of the bed and a nurse unplugged the monitor. The reassuring steady beats of the baby's heart ended, sending his own heart rate higher.

Nick followed as the orderlies rolled the bed out of the room and down the corridor. The nurse pushed the monitor, still connected to Jasmine. They entered an elevator and dropped to the second floor, turning right on exiting. He hadn't had a chance to tell Jasmine about the placenta, and after that pain had torn her up, there was no time. She would need him beside her if the test showed bad news.

They stopped inside a room with an ultrasound machine. The leading orderly shifted aside the bed already in place, and scooted Jasmine's bed into position.

The nurse plugged in the monitor, and the reassuring beat of the baby's heart returned. He hadn't realized how disturbed he'd been at the lack of the little double-thump.

He wanted to hold Jasmine's hand, but there was too much activity around her. Instead, he shifted to the end of the bed so she could see him. Her shoulders relaxed once their gazes met and as soon as the staff cleared from one side of the bed, Nick moved in and took Jasmine's hand. She gripped it hard.

He kissed her temple. "Honey, relax. Listen to our baby's heartbeat. He's okay."

Her grip loosened.

The ultrasound tech wore a nametag reading *Sherry*. She turned on the machine and adjusted dials then held up a tube of gel. "We're ready to start."

The woman folded Jasmine's blanket back and lifted the hospital gown. She spoke to the doctor. "Where do you want me to start?"

"Right here." He pointed to the area Jasmine kept rubbing. "We need to see the condition of the placenta."

Sherry spread gel on the transducer and placed it against Jasmine's belly. Nick stared at the view screen as intently as the doctor.

The doctor pointed a pen at a spot on the screen. "Stop there. The placenta has started to separate."

Jasmine clenched Nick's hand, and his heart pounded. In most of the view, the placenta was smooth and flattened at the edge, but in one place, it was puffed up.

"If that's the only place, it should be fine. Continue scanning the perimeter."

The view showed a smooth edge. Then the angle changed. Was that another separation? Nick leaned in closer.

"Stop." The doctor's pen tapped again. "I'm concerned about this."

Jasmine whimpered. Nick touched his head to hers.

The scan moved around. A greater area seemed to be thickened.

The doctor compressed his lips and stepped back. "Let's check the baby."

The technician recoated the transducer and shifted the view. The baby seemed fine. He moved a bit, his fingers flexed, and when the transducer traveled over a spot near the leg, he kicked out.

"He looks healthy. Can you take measurements?"

The doctor stepped to the bed. "I want to start you on corticosteroids. Two doses twenty-four hours apart. It will speed lung development. If we can get through forty-eight hours, the baby has a much improved chance."

Nick massaged the back of Jasmine's neck. "The baby's going to be born in forty-eight hours?"

"The goal is to go at least that long. If we can get a few

more days, all the better." The doctor rested his hand on Nick's shoulder. "Babies this age are born every day. We've got everything needed to take care of him."

It would still be a battle—one that shouldn't be happening.

Jasmine tensed. Her voice held panic. "Is he going to be all right?"

"His chances are favorable. We're moving you to the maternity floor. I want a nurse checking on you every thirty minutes for the first twenty-four hours. Hourly after that."

Jasmine glanced at Nick then back at the doctor. "What's she going to check for?"

"They'll have the heart monitor on the baby, but the nurse will check for bleeding."

Panic jolted through Nick. They could both still die. His worry had eased somewhat when Jasmine had been awake and seemed so much better, but something could go wrong at any time. He'd read of women dying from bleeding during childbirth.

The technician extended a printout. "Doctor, here are the measurements."

He took the paper and scanned the page, studied Jasmine and Nick. "Size and weight are acceptable. I won't be too concerned if we have to go early." He handed the sheet to the nurse, his eyes never leaving Jasmine. "I'll see you later today."

Once again the life line of the monitor amplifying the baby's heartbeat was disconnected, and Nick followed Jasmine's bed through the halls and into an elevator, getting off on the sixth floor. Josh stood beside a door past the nursing station, but he wasn't alone. He conversed with a petite blonde woman wearing dark pants and a light blue shirt, a badge suspended from a cord around her neck.

The orderlies rolled Jasmine's bed into her new room.

Nick stopped beside Josh.

"Nick," Josh said, "this is Detective Francine Carlisle. She's investigating the case against Dean. She needs to talk to Jasmine."

Even though Nick wanted every piece of evidence against Dean revealed, this woman wasn't getting near Jasmine in her delicate condition.

Chapter 18

Nick frowned. "I don't know if that's a good idea." He glanced at Josh. "The placenta has started to detach, so I don't want Jasmine stressed." He stared down at the detective. "I can probably answer most of your questions about the...event." He didn't want to say the words 'attempted murder'.

Detective Carlisle gave a quick nod. "I'll start with you, but I'll still need to talk to her. I'll try to keep my questions to a minimum."

She motioned for him to follow. "I saw an empty room where we can talk."

Nick looked into Jasmine's room. The nurse plugged in the baby monitor, and he waited for several beats, reassured that it sounded normal. He squeezed Josh's shoulder. "Keep an eye on her." He'd given a statement already. At this point, Jasmine was more important.

"Will do." Josh disappeared into his sister's room.

They entered an empty patient room and pulled chairs near each other then sat.

Carlisle opened her notebook. "Tell me what happened last night."

She'd likely read the statement he'd given the policeman the night before. He rehashed the event starting with hearing voices when he walked down the hall, leaving out the fact that he'd gone there to make up with Jasmine.

She squinted at him. "And why would Kennedy think a pregnant woman's suicide note would be believable?"

The officer the previous night hadn't asked. Nick stared at his clasped hands. The fear of losing Jasmine's love had hurt, but the fear of losing her to death had nearly killed him. "Because a week ago Jasmine found out I had purchased ten percent of Kennedy Holdings and hadn't told her. She broke off our engagement. I showed up last night to explain why I did it."

"A good thing you did. Are you two officially engaged again?"

He smiled. "I haven't had a chance to ask her again, but she's forgiven me."

Nick wanted to make sure all the damning evidence was together. He explained how he'd ended up outside Rhonda's office and what he'd heard between them.

She nodded. "You seem to have a knack for overhearing Dean Kennedy's conversations." Nick shrugged. "Are you also the reason Arthur Kennedy's body was exhumed?"

"Yes. I told Josh what I heard and he made it happen."

"And Jasmine knew this?"

"No."

Her eyebrows spiked up.

"We decided not to tell Jasmine until we knew for sure. After the autopsy report, Josh told Jasmine their father had been murdered, but not that we suspected Dean."

"I'd be afraid to keep that many secrets from my fiancé. If Jasmine had known, it might have saved her from almost dying."

Nick sucked in a breath. "No. It wouldn't have. Dean put the meth into Jasmine's plastic lemon. She squeezed it into her water bottle herself."

"What? I have to get that picked up." She scribbled in

her notebook.

"Jasmine told me this morning she'd broken the seal on the water bottle and guessed the meth was in her lemon. I called the officer I talked to last night, and he assured me it would be picked up."

"Let me check to be sure." Carlisle flipped a page in her notebook and punched a number in her phone. After a quick conversation she put her phone away. "Another thing. Maybe if you'd told her, she wouldn't have broken up with you and Dean Kennedy wouldn't have had a feasible reason for killing Jasmine."

Nick leaned forward, and put steel in his voice. "Then he would have found another way. I think he wanted Jasmine—" his heart ached, and he rubbed his eyes "—dead before the baby's born. Then he can eliminate Josh and inherit Kennedy Holdings."

She scribbled in her notebook. "That's a possibility I can look into."

She stood. "Now, I want to talk to Jasmine."

"I want to be there."

She shook her head. "I need to talk to her alone."

"And I need to make sure talking about this doesn't stress her. She had an ultrasound this morning and it wasn't good. We might lose the baby." Saying the words made it too real. Jasmine and the baby had to be all right.

"I'll be careful."

"Let's ask the nurse if stressful questioning might cause her to lose the baby."

Carlisle compressed her lips. "Fine. You can stay, but don't interfere."

They entered Jasmine's room. She and Josh spoke in low voices, heads close together. He straightened as Nick and the detective approached the bed.

Detective Carlisle flipped her notebook to another page.

"I need to question Miss Kennedy. Mr., ah, Josh, you'll have to leave."

"Is Nick staying?" Worry marred Josh's forehead.

"Yes," Nick said.

"Good." Josh kissed Jasmine's head. "See you later, sis." He joined Nick at the foot of the bed. "The nurse put that steroid in Jasmine's IV. The one for the baby's lungs."

Nick nodded. He hoped it worked. After Josh left, Nick stepped to the side of the bed and took Jasmine's hand, then waited for Detective Carlisle to begin.

~~~

Jasmine closed her eyes. She couldn't believe how tiring it had been talking to Detective Carlisle. She ran a hand over her belly, trying to sooth the ache that told her there was still something wrong.

The detective's questions had made her remember details about the night before that she hadn't wanted to think about, or at least hadn't wanted to associate with her uncle.

Josh hadn't liked Uncle Dean for a long time, but she'd felt sorry for him. She assumed most of his bad behavior was connected to Aunt Pam and the children's leaving him seven years before. Now she wondered if Aunt Pam had left because she knew Uncle Dean could be dangerous.

The chair next to her bed squeaked. Nick had stood beside her as her silent sentinel, holding her hand the whole time the detective questioned her. A couple of times he started to speak, but Carlisle glared at him, and he stopped. He'd probably been afraid the detective would send him out of the room.

She smiled at him. "Thanks for being here with me."

He leaned close to her. "I couldn't be anywhere else. It would drive me crazy not knowing for sure you were okay."

Tears filled her eyes, and she blinked them away. "I love you. I don't deserve you after the way I mistrusted you."

He gave her a gentle kiss and settled back in the chair. "Honey, I don't blame you. I did it all wrong. I still want us to get married."

This time she couldn't keep the tears from spilling over. "Me, too. I've been so miserable without you."

He reached into his pocket. "In that case—" he opened his hand with her engagement ring on his palm "—will you wear this again?"

She held out her hand. "Oh, Nick. Yes."

He slipped the ring on her finger and lightly rubbed her belly. "The baby will be in your arms instead of in your belly for the wedding."

She giggled. "Finding a dress might be easier."

His eyes took on a haunted expression. "I have one more thing to confess."

It couldn't be worse than what they'd already gone through. She took a big breath and let it out slowly. "Um, okay."

"I might lose Lawson Prime Secure. You could end up marrying an unemployed programmer."

"What? Why?"

"To get the rest of the money to buy into Kennedy Holdings, I put up fifty percent of my company as collateral. The first income payment from Kennedy Holdings wasn't enough to cover my monthly loan payment. I'll only be able to cover the full payments for a few months."

Losing a company he'd built himself would be worse than her losing ten percent of her family's company. And he'd done it for her. "But I saw the statement. The income payment seemed quite substantial." She couldn't let him lose his dreams and hard work. "I can cover the rest."

"The statement you gave Matt showed the income

payment I should have received, which would have been more than enough. The actual one I got, and the check they sent, had a much lower payment."

Jasmine tilted her head. Maybe that was why Uncle Dean had tried to kill her. So she wouldn't find out he was embezzling. "I don't know why he sold a piece of the company to begin with since we had enough reserves already. The money hasn't even been touched. You know what? We can return fourteen million so you can pay the loan off. Your ownership will be five instead of ten percent."

He frowned. "The loan is fifteen million."

She shook her head. "Half of twenty-eight million is fourteen."

"I paid a total of thirty million."

Her eyes widened. "Oh, my, God. He stole two million dollars. I wonder if we can get it back. Can you call Detective Carlisle about it? That's got to strengthen the case against him."

Nick gripped her shoulders, and leaned close. "Jasmine, calm down. Take some deep breaths with me."

She hadn't realized how tense she'd gotten until then. She breathed in with him and out. Over and over, staring into his concerned eyes. Her shoulders relaxed and the knot in her stomach unwound.

Nick rubbed his cheek against hers. "Don't scare me like that. I'm calling the nurse to check you."

Chapter 19

The watery eggs and soggy toast weren't appealing. Lucky for Jasmine the sausages were tasty. Since she was recovering, she really had to eat. She waved her fork with a chunk of meat on it. "Are you sure you don't want a sausage link?"

Nick sat in a chair next to her bed. "I'm fine. I'll grab something in the cafeteria after Josh comes."

The night before, the nurse had slowly raised the head of the bed making it easier to eat dinner. Again this morning, a nurse raised her bed, then checked to make sure there was no bleeding.

Josh strolled in with a smile and a large brown paper bag.

Nick's eyebrows rose. "Oh, you've got food."

She eyed the bag. Mmm. There was a new, tantalizing scent. "Yeah. What do you have?"

Josh set his bag on the foot of her bed. "Breakfast. Lydia made it. She fussed about how bad hospital food was and said she had to make you a decent breakfast."

She sniffed. "Is that...cinnamon?" She flexed her fingers in a give-me gesture. "Did she make her cinnamon coffee cake?"

"Yes." He set a paper plate with the cake covered in plastic wrap on her tray, then removed a stack of paper plates, and smirked. "Don't forget to give Nick a piece."

She caught Nick's smile. He hadn't had it before. It'd be a treat he wouldn't forget.

Josh fumbled in the bag and lifted out an aluminum pie plate.

Jasmine grinned. "Is that ham quiche?" She was glad the egg problem had ended after the first four months.

"Yes."Josh cut the coffee cake and quiche, loading it onto three plates, and handed one with a plastic fork to Nick and settled into the second chair with his own plate.

Jasmine scooped up a piece of cake. "Mmm. I'm giving Lydia a kiss the next time I see her." Except for the sausages, the hospital breakfast was far from acceptable.

She waited until they were finished eating to ask Josh about the board meeting, not wanting Nick's meal spoiled.

A nurse bustled in. "Let's check you."

"Hi, Andrea."

The nurse checked for bleeding, then took Jasmine's blood pressure, and temperature. "Everything's fine. Let's give you the second dose of corticosteroid." She pulled a syringe from her pocket, checked its label and injected it into Jasmine's IV. "I'll see you in a bit."

Jasmine relaxed against her pillow. "All right, Josh. Is it all set up?"

Nick narrowed his eyes at Jasmine before turning to Josh.

Her brother stretched out his arms, as if waiting for applause. "Yes. I called a meeting of the board. It's this afternoon. I'm marching into the board room as soon as they're seated and demanding to be voted in as the CEO. I'll glare at every one of them and ask if there are objections."

This action seemed too bold. Jasmine didn't want her brother disappointed again. "Aren't you afraid the ones who voted you out before will still be against you?"

"No. Well, not all of them. I had Rhonda send the board members a report yesterday with all the embezzlement evidence we could find. That'll convince them they made a poor choice before. In the meeting, I'll inform them that I'm bringing in an outside accounting firm to comb the books for the past five years, looking for any improprieties." He squeezed Jasmine's leg through the blanket. "And I'll tell them that Dean tried to kill you."

Nick took her hand. She glanced at him, at the concern on his face. Something bad was happening.

Josh stared into her eyes. "And that he probably killed Dad."

She tightened her grip on Nick's hand. Her heart twisted. "Uncle Dean killed Dad? How could he do that to his own brother?"

Nick stood, leaned over and pressed his cheek to hers.

Josh rubbed her leg again. "How could he do this to his favorite niece?" His voice broke.

Josh closed his eyes for a few seconds. "My first order of business will be to pay off Nick's bank loan. I'll recommend they let him keep the full ten percent, seeing how he was trying to keep the company together, but I won't pressure them."

Nick straightened up. "It's not necessary to keep it at ten percent."

Josh held out his hand, and Nick shook it. "I know, but you took a big risk for Jasmine. For us." His eyes misted over. "I'll be forever grateful you saved her life."

Seeing her brother's emotions prompted her own tears.

Nick's other arm rounded Josh's shoulder, a sort of man hug. "I'll be proud to have you for a brother-in-law."

Josh stepped back. "So the wedding's back on?"

Jasmine grinned and held up her ringed hand.

Nick smiled at her. "Yes. The day is dependent on when

157

the baby comes home from the hospital. I want my family present."

Josh slapped Nick on the back. "I'm glad you two worked it out. Well, I'm out of here. I've got a meeting to prepare for."

After Josh left, Jasmine eyed Nick. "Don't you have work to do?"

"I worked while you slept."

"But you haven't left since you got here. Don't you want to go home and shower? Put on clean clothes?"

He kissed her nose. "Are you trying to tell me I stink?"

She chuckled. "No. I wish I could have a shower, so I figured you would want one, too."

His face sobered, and he took her hand. "Honey, I don't want to leave in case something happens with the baby. I'm not letting you face that alone."

How had she thought Nick didn't love her and was using her? In her pain and panic, she'd so misjudged him. "I love you. I'm sorry I didn't trust in you."

"You already apologized. And I'm the one at fault. I should have told you about the sale before I placed my first bid."

"But—" He covered her mouth with a finger.

"It's over. We're starting fresh." He kissed her. Not one of the hot ones she really liked, but one still filled with love.

She relaxed against the pillow. "We still have to name the baby."

He smiled. "Good idea while we have all this time. Any suggestions?"

"I'd like his middle name to be Arthur after my father."

"Okay. How about a first name of…George or Harold or Felix or—"

She giggled and nudged him. "Be serious."

"How about Blaine? It's my dad's middle name."

She tipped her head. "Blaine Arthur Lawson. I like it." She kissed him. "You know, some couples have huge fights over naming their baby."

"We can fight over the next one."

She poked him. "Nick! Why would we want to argue about it?"

He wiggled his eyebrows. "Because making up is supposed to be fun."

She sighed. "That hasn't worked out so well for us. We made up from our first fight, and I-I'm in the hospital." She'd almost said she nearly died, but didn't want to remind him.

~~~

Nick's fingers flew over his laptop keyboard, hammering out the new idea he had for his program. Jasmine lay curled on her side in the hospital bed next to his chair. She'd fallen asleep shortly after dinner. He glanced up at the squeak of shoes on the tile.

Josh was back.

Nick put a finger to his lips and tipped his head toward Jasmine.

Josh nodded and sat in the empty chair. "Do you want to go home and shower now?" he whispered.

It would be the first time leaving Jasmine since she woke up from the drug three days ago. He was afraid to leave. Staying with her, he couldn't control what happened, but he could give Jasmine his support, and he'd know about every health problem the instant it cropped up.

His eyes stayed on Jasmine. "I'm not sure if I should leave."

"I'm staying until you get back. If anything comes up, I'll call and you can be back in ten minutes."

It would be longer than ten minutes, but Jasmine had

done well that day.

Her eyes fluttered, then opened. "Hi."

Nick leaned close and ran his fingers over her cheek. "Hi, yourself. How do you feel?"

"Okay, I guess. Can you raise the head of the bed?"

He pushed the button and the head slowly rose. He stopped. "How's that?"

"A little bit more." Her eyes brightened as they alighted on her brother. "Josh. How was the meeting?"

He grinned, stood and bowed. "You're looking at the reinstated CEO."

Jasmine clapped. "They went along with it. What else?"

Josh reseated himself and glanced at Nick. "You'll get a check next week for half of what you actually paid to the company, *and* you'll retain seven percent ownership. Before they give you the check, you'll have to sign an agreement that if you and Jasmine split up, you will either be reimbursed for the other half in two installments, one year apart, or you give your share to Jasmine or your joint children."

Nick nodded. "I don't have a problem with that. Thanks for going to bat for me." He'd planned on gifting his share of the company to Jasmine as a wedding present anyway.

Josh settled back in his chair. "I like Matt. We had a long conversation after the meeting ended. Now that your secret is out, are you going to keep him on the board or take over?"

Nick glanced at Jasmine. "I'd planned on taking over, but I think I'll leave Matt in place for a while. He *does* have a boat he wants to buy."

"Good enough." Josh waved toward the door. "Why don't you take off now? I can have a nice conversation with my sister."

Nick leaned closer to her. "Will you be okay for a bit?"

"I've got Josh. I'm sure you could use a break from me."

He stood and kissed her. "I'll never need a break from

you."

Chapter 20

Jasmine woke in partial darkness, and to the reassuring beat of the baby's heart on the monitor. She wished she could stretch her arms, body, anything, but was afraid to because of the placenta problem. The door was almost closed, muffling the never ending sounds on the hospital floor—babies crying, whispered voices, the swish of nurses' shoes on the tile, an occasional clatter.

There. That's what woke her. A woman cried out in pain. Probably having a normal delivery. That wouldn't be her. Not after what Uncle Dean had done. She could have spent these last few weeks getting ready for her baby—buying furniture and clothes, being excited and happy. Instead, she worried that her son might die. All because a man got greedy and didn't care who he destroyed to get money.

Dr. Connors had come in and reviewed her test and treatment. She'd told her the only option was a c-section. There was too much chance of the placenta detaching during labor, risking both their lives.

They'd take it day by day, and the doctor hoped she'd go another week. Jasmine wasn't happy about being in the hospital for that long. After the tensions and worry of the first day, these past three days had become tedious, but if it gave her baby a chance to mature further, she'd do it for a month.

Jasmine gazed at Nick's silhouette in the dull light

creeping between the slats in the blinds. He lay curled in the too short, cushioned window seat. He said it was more comfortable than the chair he'd slept in the first night.

He'd been her rock. She didn't know how she could have believed he didn't love her. It was in every glance, touch and word.

Her hip hurt. She wished she could turn over on her own, but it put too much strain on her abdomen. She sighed and closed her eyes. Maybe she could go back to sleep.

"Honey, you okay?" Nick dropped his feet to the floor and sat up.

"Just a sore hip. Sorry to wake you."

"I was trying to decide if I should get up. It's nearly seven." He stretched his arms over his head. She wished she could do that.

He crossed the room and kissed her forehead. "Do you want to sit up or roll over?" He'd become an expert at helping her turn.

"Sit up. Josh should be here with breakfast soon." Josh had promised before leaving to have Lydia make breakfast again. After the meal, he'd go to work.

She was excited for Josh. He'd moped the first week after he'd been fired. Being the son of the owner, unless he royally screwed up, he should have had a job for life. But not with Uncle Dean in charge. Josh hadn't been surprised, but she'd been blindsided.

In the end, Josh studied investing, going beyond what their father had taught him. Maybe, given time, he would have learned more from their dad. Now he was going into Kennedy Holdings stronger than when he left. She was proud of her brother.

Nick helped her shift to her back, then raised the head of the bed. That position was much more comfortable.

Someone caught Nick's attention at the door, and he

smiled. Josh must have arrived.

Her nurse rounded the curtain. No breakfast yet. "How are you this morning, Jasmine?"

"I'm okay." She'd try not to complain. Her baby's heart continued to beat, and that was worth all of her discomfort.

"Let's check you out, and I'll get out of here." The nurse's first checks in the morning were quick since she saw all her patients.

Josh entered while a thermometer was still in Jasmine's mouth. She wiggled her fingers at him. He greeted everyone with a smile.

The nurse removed the thermometer. "Everything's good. See you later, Jasmine."

"Bye, Andrea."

Josh stepped to the side, allowing Andrea to pass, then set his bag on the tray table. "Lydia made some kind of omelet burrito wraps today."

"Oh, that sounds good." Lydia must have been experimenting.

He removed plates from the bag, placed two wax paper wrapped burritos on each, and passed them out.

Josh and Nick took their usual seats.

Jasmine unwrapped a burrito. "Josh, was your second day better than your first?" The morning before he'd regaled her with stories of his first day back. Most of it had been spent in individual meetings with upper management. He'd needed to get up to speed on investment plans, but he'd also wanted to scope out loyalties.

"Somewhat. I had a couple group meetings. Most people seemed enthusiastic about my new strategies." He'd had months to plan out what he would change if he took control at Kennedy Holdings.

Jasmine was all for it. If only he could have worked with their dad to implement it. "Dad would have loved your new ideas. I'm so glad you're back."

"Not everybody is. I had to fire Troy Jarvis."

She gasped, inhaling food. Troy had worked his way up to manage his own division. He'd been with the company for over fifteen years.

She gulped down some water. It didn't help. She bent forward as she coughed, took a couple sips of water and coughed more. Pain seared her side, and she pressed against it with her hand.

"Uhh!" She shoved the table away so she could curl her legs up. When the placenta had pulled away before, it had hurt, but this was excruciating. She panted, trying to control the pain, trying to calm down, hoping less stress would help the baby.

Nick and Josh leaped to their feet.

Nick hovered over her, probably afraid to touch her. "Honey, what's wrong?"

"Jasmine! I'm so sorry." Josh hovered behind Nick.

Andrea rushed in. Nick must have pushed the call button. "Move aside!" She peeked under the sheet. "You're bleeding." Her gaze flew to the monitor. "The baby's heartbeat is still good, but I'm calling the doctor." She hurried out.

Jasmine stared at the monitor as she rubbed circles over the painful spot. Her little guy was still getting oxygen, but maybe his moving at this point could dislodge the fragile placenta. It should have been days more before the c-section. Her baby had to survive. Tears trickled from her eyes, the emotional agony far worse than the physical pain.

Nick stroked her hair and kissed her forehead. "I wish I could do something for you." Just having him near—having his strength—helped. Whatever happened, they could weather it together.

Andrea returned with two orderlies. "We're taking her to

surgery. The doctor will meet us there."

Jasmine grabbed Nick's hand. She didn't want the baby taken already. He could hold on longer. The heart monitor still beat regularly.

Nick bent over the rail. "We'll do what we have to do, honey. We're going to get through this. All three of us."

She nodded. Another pain hit, and she groaned, curling up tighter. Without Uncle Dean, she'd be blissfully anticipating the birth of her healthy child in five weeks. Now, she might lose the son she already loved.

The steady heartbeats on the monitor ended.

"No!" She buried her face into the pillow.

Nick touched her cheek. "Jasmine. They just unplugged the monitor. The baby's still okay."

She bit her lip. But they wouldn't know if the beats changed while they moved her. The baby might start struggling on her way to the operating room and nobody would know until it was too late.

"Please, hurry." Maybe she said it too quietly. "Please, Hurry!"

The bed moved toward the door, and Andrea patted Jasmine's shoulder. "We're on our way. We'll get you hooked up again in no time."

They rolled past the elevators where the sudden plunge might worsen the placenta separation. They pushed her into a large, bright room, and placed the bed near an operating table.

"Let's move her," Andrea said.

Jasmine stiffened, waiting for the pain.

They slipped a board under her, and three pairs of hands shifted her onto the table without causing her additional pain.

An orderly plugged in the monitor. Jasmine's shoulders dropped when the thump-thump resumed on the speaker.

Nick moved in beside her and took her hand. "I'm right

166

here until they kick me out."

Her heart plummeted. She needed him. "Kick you out?"

A hand touched her shoulder. "Jasmine. I'm the anesthesiologist, Dr. Risemann. I'm giving you a spinal block."

"Okay."

"You have to stay really still."

She nodded. She'd waited days with nothing happening, but now everything came in a rush of people preparing, pain, and fear. And Nick wouldn't be with her.

"Look at me, honey." Nick held Jasmine's shoulder. "They won't let me stay because this is an emergency, but I'm here right now. Concentrate on me."

He became blurry, and she blinked, a weak attempt to sharpen her vision. "Nick, I'm scared." A sharp pain stung her back, and she closed her eyes, concentrating on keeping still.

Dr. Risemann patted her hip. "There we go. You did great."

The pain was gone, and she relaxed her tense shoulders. The lack of pain almost seemed like a bad thing since she wouldn't know if the problem with the placenta got worse.

Nick kissed her forehead. "Honey, these people are experts. They've done this hundreds of times."

"I love you."

He kissed her. "I love you, too."

The doctor entered with his gloved hands held carefully in front of him. "Clear out non-essentials."

Nick glanced over his shoulder and back to her. "I have to go, but I'll see you as soon as they let me in."

He trudged away, but turned back for a second at the door. He mouthed the words, "I love you."

This might be the last time she saw him. There was a risk both she and the baby would die. She couldn't hold back the tears at the pain Nick would suffer. She'd fight harder than ever to survive because he needed her.

Something was different. She let her senses pickup everything around her. The heartbeat. "The baby's heartbeat is different." Nobody responded to her, not even Nick who was walking out the operating room door.

She wasn't sure if it was faster or slower than before, she just knew it had changed. Louder this time, with panic. "The baby's heartbeat is different!"

Nick jerked his head around, his stricken expression hidden as the door shut.

Chapter 21

Josh pulled on his arm before Nick pushed through the door. "You'll be in the way. She needs the doctor right now."

Nick yanked away. "Jasmine said there's something wrong!" She was alone and worried about the health of their baby.

Josh dragged him back, his tone firmer. "And they'll do everything possible for her, Nick."

Nick jerked his arm away from Josh's hold. He sighed and ran his hand through his hair.

Josh swallowed. "Come on. Let's have a seat in the waiting room. It's right around the corner. They'll know where to find us."

Nick followed Josh and stood in the center of the small room. Cushioned chairs line three walls, and a TV hung on the wall beside the door. He couldn't sit still while Jasmine went through the pain and fear of surgery.

Josh dropped a hand on Nick's shoulder. "I am so sorry what I said set off that coughing spell. Jasmine wouldn't be in there right now if I hadn't told her about Troy."

Nick shook his head. "It was bound to happen. The doctor figured it would be any day."

"Still, I'm sorry I made it this day." Josh sat in a cushioned chair, leaning forward with elbows on his knees.

Nick paced.

Several minutes passed, and Josh groaned. "You're making me dizzy. Sit down."

"I can't."

He crossed to the water dispenser and filled a cup, gulping it down, then half filled it and splashed it over his face. He sat in a chair on the opposite side of the room from Josh, and tipped his head from side to side, trying to relax his tense muscles. His legs tingled and he bounced them. It wasn't enough. He jumped up and paced again.

He couldn't imagine how, for hundreds of years, men had stayed outside while their wives delivered babies. Next time, he would be with her. And he'd be by her side right from the moment they found out she was pregnant.

"I'm glad she has you."

Nick stopped pacing.

Josh gave him a half smile. "Not only because you saved her life. I don't think anyone could love her more than you do."

"Thanks." Josh's words calmed him enough that he could sit. He bent over, hands clasped, feet tapping, staring at a spot of dried coffee on the floor.

"Jasmine Kennedy's family?" The doctor stood in the doorway.

"Yes," Nick and Josh said together, and jumped to their feet.

"Jasmine's fine. She came through the c-section well, no excessive bleeding. The baby…"

Nick tensed at the pause. *No, don't say he didn't make it.* His eyes watered, and he blinked it away.

"The baby is in NICU. He's breathing on his own, but we've got him on oxygen. We have to maintain his body temperature. He weighed in at four pounds, seven ounces. Not bad for his age."

He was alive. "He's going to be all right?"

"His chances are good. We've had younger, smaller babies do just fine. He'll have to stay in NICU for at least two weeks."

"Can we see them?" Josh asked.

"One at a time in the recovery room in about twenty minutes or so. Someone will come out."

"When can we see the baby?" Nick asked. Jasmine and their son were alive.

"You can see him through the window now." He pointed down the hall. "He's in the second nursery. You won't be able to touch him until he's stabilized."

"We can't pick him up?"

"I'm sorry, not at this time. The nurse in NICU will go over the procedures." He turned and strode down the hall.

Relief coursed through Nick as he hurried down the corridor, his legs as rubbery as Jello. He'd focused on hope and willing them to live, but hadn't been able to keep the fear away. The twisting pain in his gut unknotted and dissolved. "They made it."

~~~

Jasmine rubbed her hand over her flabby stomach, careful not to tug the stitches. The searing pain of the detaching placenta was gone, replaced with the dull throb of her incisions.

The little life inside her was gone, growing stronger in the NICU. His weak cry when Dr. Young had removed him from her body had worried her, but the doctor said other babies who didn't cry when they were born had survived.

She wished she could hold him again. They'd cleaned and dressed him, and strung an oxygen tube under his nose. Then they placed him in her arms. She kissed and talk to him, then touched his little hand and her heart swelled when he gripped her finger. Her little guy was a fighter. After a couple of minutes, the nurse apologized and took him away.

"Hey, there." Nick's voice.

Her gaze flew to his face, and she held out her hand.

He hurried to her side and grasped it, kissing her forehead. "I saw him. He's so tiny."

She nodded. "They let me hold him for a couple of minutes."

"That's good, right? If something was wrong, they wouldn't have let you." He brushed the hair back from her face. "How are you feeling?"

She sighed. "I'm okay. I'm glad that's over, but not. I wish I'd been able to carry him to term."

He rubbed noses with her. "Next time you will. I'm glad you're both okay. Josh had to hold me back when you yelled about the baby's heartbeat."

Poor Nick. "Sorry. It turned out to be nothing serious."

A nurse arrived. "This is the dad?"

Jasmine didn't take her eyes from Nick. "Yes."

"Okay." She pulled a hospital band from her pocket. "We have to band you so you can see the baby. You'll have to show this to get near him." She compared the numbers on it with the one on Jasmine's wrist, then snapped it onto Nick's wrist. She smiled at Jasmine. "You ready to change visitors? There's an anxious brother out here."

Nick kissed Jasmine. "I'll see you in a bit."

As Nick and Josh passed, Josh squeezed Nick's shoulder. "Congrats, Dad."

Nick grinned.

Josh kissed her cheek. "I was so worried. You look so much better than the last time I saw you." He pulled up a chair. "How do you feel, little Momma?"

Wow. She hadn't thought about it, but one day, her son would call her mom. "A lot better." She touched her belly.

"I've got pain from the surgery, but I'm not as worried about the baby. The doctors can access him instantly if he has a problem."

"I wish we could have jumped on this sooner with Uncle Dean. If I'd known he'd try to kill you, I would have insisted the police arrest him a while ago. We—Nick and I—knew he killed Dad, but there wasn't evidence to prove it." His voice turned hard. "Now, there's plenty of evidence to put him away."

"You didn't go into the office today."

He squeezed her hand. "Family's more important. I'll go in a few minutes, now I know you're okay."

Andrea entered the room. "It's time to go back to your room, Jasmine. Then you can have two handsome visitors at once."

Josh chuckled and stood. "Unfortunately, this visitor is going to work." He kissed Jasmine's forehead. "See you later, sis."

"Bye, Josh."

Andrea checked Jasmine's vitals and removed the IV. Jasmine flexed her arm. "Oh, that feels good."

"I thought you might like to see your son."

On cue, an orderly brought a wheelchair. "Here you go."

"I can get out of bed?" It seemed more like weeks than days since she last stood.

Andrea wheeled the chair close to the bed and set the brakes. "In a couple days, you can walk a little to see him."

The nurse helped Jasmine into the chair. It turned out to be harder than she expected—painful and she was so weak she shook.

Andrea wheeled Jasmine into the hallway.

Nick had been leaning against the opposite wall. He bent down. His lips aimed for her forehead, but she tipped her head up and got a kiss on her nose.

He chuckled and changed his aim, kissing her lips. "Honey, you look wonderful."

Andrea pushed her three doors down and stopped. "Let me see how the baby's doing." She entered the nursery

Nick stepped to the window. "His eyes are open."

Jasmine sighed. "I wish I could see."

He stared down at her in the chair, maybe gauging if he could pick her up without hurting her.

Andrea opened the door. "We're going in to see your little guy." She wheeled Jasmine into the NICU and Nick followed. They stopped in front of a sink. "Wash your hands. Both of you."

"We get to touch him?" Jasmine asked.

"Yes."

After their hands were clean, the nurse helped Jasmine to her feet. "There you go."

The baby lay in a clear plastic box with two holes in the front. A small feeding tube holding donated breast milk extended into one nostril. His skin was flushed red.

"Reach in and rub his back." Andrea said.

Jasmine tentatively snaked her hand through a hole and touched her baby, and gently rubbed. She'd forgotten how smooth and soft his skin was. He closed his eyes, as if he liked it. "Open your eyes little Blaine. I want you to see us."

"You can reach through the other opening, Nick," Andrea said.

Nick rested a hand on Jasmine's back as he reached through the second hole to touch their son. She'd had a chance to hold him, but this would be the first touch for Nick. He skimmed the baby's leg and ran his hand down to the heel. She took his hand and moved it up to the baby's back as she rubbed the arm.

She gazed up at Nick, swooning at the intense love on his face. She couldn't ask for a more loving man for her son's father.

"He's beautiful." He kissed her temple. "I loved him when I felt him kick, but this. To touch him and see him…he's a part of us."

Andrea rested her hand on the top of the isolette. "Babies need a lot of touching, and that's not always possible in the NICU, so anytime you want to come in, and there's not an emergency here, you're welcome to touch him. And talk, too."

They spent several minutes getting to know their son. The best part was the relief that he had survived.

Chapter 22

Nick marched into the police station and approached a woman with a dark, short haircut, sitting at the main desk. "I'm Nick Lawson. Detective Carlisle is expecting me." This seemed a waste of time. He'd given his statement and didn't have any new information.

"She's expecting you." The woman pointed to her right. "Her office is the third door on the left."

"Thanks."

He stopped in front of the detective's open door. Her head was bent over a pile of papers. Today, her hair was down, shoulder length, instead of in the ponytail like last time. He cleared his throat

She raised her head. "Come on in, Mr. Lawson."

He wondered if she conducted most of her interviews seated. Being so short, she must be at a disadvantage while interrogating suspects. Her desk was cleared except for a neat stack of file folders to her left and an open one in front of her.

"Call me Nick." He sat in the chair in front of her desk and rested his hands on his knees. "Did you get my voicemail about possible embezzlement?"

"Yes. We're checking into it. Can you give us a copy of your agreement with Kennedy Holdings?"

"I'll have my lawyer get it to you by tomorrow morning, as well as copies of the monthly statements I received from

Jasmine and Dean Kennedy."

"Thanks. Now the reason I called you in…" She studied him for endless seconds. "When did you and Jasmine meet?"

"What? What does that have to do with Dean trying to kill her?" It seemed like a left field question. But, he had to admit part of what bothered him about the question was that it required an awkward answer. It didn't put him in a good light to have gone to bed with a woman who didn't remember it afterward. He rarely thought about it now that Jasmine knew.

"Dean Kennedy said you and Jasmine met months before Arthur Kennedy died. That the two of you planned his death together."

With each word, Nick's anger mounted, but he tamped it down. He couldn't defend himself if he didn't think straight.

The detective leaned forward. "And that it was you who tried to kill Jasmine. He sounded pretty broken up over her brush with death."

"That's ridiculous. He's trying to wiggle out of murder and attempted murder charges. Arthur's death would still be considered a heart attack if I hadn't told Josh what I overheard. Why would I suggest exhuming the body if I were guilty?"

"That makes sense, but you held Jasmine's hand the entire time I questioned her."

"She nearly died, and you made her relive it." His voice had risen, and he paused to regain some control. "She needed my support."

"Or, you squeezed her hand a little too hard if you thought she'd answer incorrectly."

"What?" His gut churned at the thought anyone would think he'd do something like that. "That's just crazy." He ran a hand through his hair. "Go talk to her without me. She had the baby this morning, so you won't stress her into losing him now. Only, all her thoughts will be on our little guy in the NICU and if he'll make it."

"Since it was suggested, I have to ask. When did you meet Jasmine?" She did sound as if it was routine, and not an accusation.

He leaned back. "Fine. We met on the evening of her father's funeral. She was in the bar at my hotel."

"Hotel? Why were you staying at a hotel?"

"I didn't live in New York at that time. I was here on business."

Carlisle leaned back and crossed her arms. "Go on."

"She looked sad, and I wanted to cheer her up, so I sat down at the table across from her to talk." It still bothered him she'd been drunker than he'd thought.

The detective studied him. "So, you contacted her afterward?"

He shook his head. "We only exchanged first names. I didn't know how to find her." He recounted how he'd found Jasmine again.

She tapped a finger on the arm of her chair. "So, you didn't know Arthur Kennedy or Josh Kennedy before that night with Jasmine?"

"No." Nick hoped his truth was more believable than Dean's lies.

"I still need to talk to her."

"She'll tell you the same story because it's the truth. Now I have a question. Are you going to hold Dean without bail? I'm afraid he'll try to hurt Jasmine if you release him."

She scribbled on one of her pages. "We haven't finished determining charges, but I'll advise the DA of your concerns."

"Thanks. Are we through?" The faster he got out of there, the sooner he could take care of business and return to Jasmine.

She stood. "That covers it for now. Don't forget to send me those papers."

"I'll be on it as soon as I'm out of here." He'd do anything to ensure Dean spent a long time behind bars.

~~~

Jasmine glanced up from her book, a gift from Anna. "Nick!" She set the book aside. It seemed like so long since he'd left that morning. She'd missed his presence after the days he'd been with her.

He gave her a kiss on the cheek. "Hi, honey. You look so much more rested."

"I feel a lot better. I have so much to tell you. I got to try to feed the baby today. He wasn't strong enough, but I got to feed him my milk from a bottle. We had skin-to-skin contact. It was so nice. I can't wait for you to hold him."

He chuckled. "Do I have to take my shirt off to do it?"

She giggled. "No. You can just unbutton it." Jasmine had a sudden thought about holding their baby after they left the hospital. They lived separately, but would be married soon. They hadn't discussed where they'd live.

He sat on the edge of the bed. "Hey, what's wrong?"

She twined her hand into his and stared at them. "Are you going to live with us?"

He took her hands. "I'm living wherever you and Blaine are. Since my apartment is only a one-bedroom, and I'm subletting it, it's easy enough to give up."

She gazed into his eyes. "Josh took over the third floor, so we won't bother him too much. And whenever he decides to get married, we could find our own place." Josh wouldn't have much time for a social life while he whipped Kennedy Holdings back into shape.

Nick kissed her cheek. "Then the question is, do I move

in when you get out of the hospital or after Blaine does?"

She grinned. "When I do." It would be perfect.

Then thoughts of her earlier visitor infuriated her all over again. "Detective Carlisle came in. You know, she tried to make it sound like *you* killed Dad. I straightened her out on that."

He rubbed her arm. "I'm sorry you had to put up with her speculation. I'd hoped she'd gotten past it after I talked to her."

"What? She didn't believe you? She's going into Kennedy Holdings today to talk to some of the employees, including Rhonda. A forensic accountant will be there for a few days checking out the company finances. I told Josh she could use my office. She said they're going through Uncle Dean's finances, too. Hopefully, they'll find all the money he stole."

"I only care if it gives him a longer sentence." He wrapped a hand around the back of her neck and kissed her. "I want you to stay safe from him."

She lay back on the pillow and smiled. "Enough of that." They needed a distraction from those morbid thoughts. "Let's go see Blaine."

His eyes lit up. "I'd like that."

"Can you get a wheelchair from the nurses' station? I'm not allowed to walk until tomorrow."

"All right. I'll be back in a minute."

Nick swirled into the room, looking like an excited toddler about to pick out a puppy. "Here we go." He helped her into the chair then race walked down the corridor, past staff and visitors, to the NICU.

She clutched the armrests and giggled. "You're going to get a speeding ticket."

He stopped in front of the NICU door. "We have somewhere important to be."

The door opened, and Jasmine held out her wrist to the nurse, Alice. Nick stuck out his arm.

Alice checked the numbers on both their bands. "Come on in." They followed her to Blaine's isolette, and she checked the band around the baby's ankle. "Ready to hold the baby?"

Jasmine clasped her hands. "Let Nick hold him first." She wanted him to get bonding time since he wouldn't be able to spend as much time at the hospital.

"All right, Dad. Pull up that chair. Skin-to-skin contact is important for preemies. Wash your hands and then reveal those pecs."

Jasmine almost giggled at Nick's widened eyes. He worked the buttons loose on his shirt. She wondered if the same thoughts flashed through his head as hers. The last time they'd made love she'd been the one to unfasten his buttons.

He yanked the shirt from his pants and finished the last two buttons. She couldn't resist. She hooked her fingers into a belt loop, tugged him closer and planted a kiss on his stomach.

Alice cleared her throat. "It's not the time to make another baby."

Jasmine's face warmed, and Nick chuckled then whispered in her ear. "I love you." He nipped her earlobe, and she gasped at the tingle that zipped through her.

He washed his hands, then sat in the chair.

Alice opened the isolette, donned fresh gloves and gently lifted Blaine, careful of the tube in his nostril. She placed him in Nick's arms, and Jasmine teared up at the adoration on his face.

The baby's eyes opened, and Nick grinned. He rubbed Blaine's cheek. "Nice to meet you, little Blaine." He glanced at her, but only for a second, his gaze returning to his son. "He's so tiny."

Blaine had been small in her arms, but in Nick's he seemed to shrink. Nick cradled his son against his bare chest as if he were an ancient protector of his family.

Chapter 23

Jasmine couldn't contain her happiness. She whirled around the foyer as she waited for Nick to come downstairs, just as she'd done as a child while waiting for her parents when they had special plans. No plans could be more special than bringing home their baby three weeks after his birth.

Between visits to the hospital over the last two weeks, they'd had Blaine's room painted a pale blue, hung darker blue curtains printed with sailboats and laid out colorful area rugs. She'd had fun shopping for the white baby furniture.

Nick chuckled as he jogged down the stairs and swept her up, continuing her dance. "I love you. Are you ready to bring our son home?"

She threw her arms around his neck and her incision twinged only a bit. "Yes!"

She picked up her purse and carry-all bag, they headed out to Nick's car. She glanced into the back at the carseat Nick had installed the week before. She'd read the instructions for the base installation as Nick followed along. He'd installed an identical seat in her car.

They drove in normal traffic, but it seemed to take forever. Then Nick turned into the hospital parking lot. "I'll drop you at the door and find a parking spot."

"I can walk."

He glared. "I'm dropping you at the door."

She smiled at his overprotectiveness. He'd rented a wheelchair for her to use on their long shopping trips to buy baby clothes and furniture.

He stopped at the entrance, and she slid out. She sat on a bench near the drop-off spot and as Nick wound down one aisle and another. He parked and headed her way, carrying the baby seat. She stood as he approached and took his other hand.

She'd been so excited, and now that the time to take Blaine home was almost here, fear grabbed her. He was still so tiny and would be totally Nick's and her responsibility. The doctors and nurses took care of preemies everyday with all kinds of medical technology available if anything went wrong.

Nick stopped, set down the seat, and swung around in front of her. "Hey, what's wrong?" He rested a hand on her shoulder and rubbed her jaw with his thumb. It was amazing how he sensed her moods.

She bit her lip. "I'm afraid Blaine will get sick, and we won't know what to do."

"Honey, he's fine, or they wouldn't let him go home. And we're only a call away from the best medical care."

She lifted her shoulders and dropped them. "I'm being silly, aren't I?"

He wrapped his arms around her. "You're being a first time mom." He leaned back and gazed at her. "You love him and want to make sure he's in good hands. And he is."

"How come you're not nervous?"

"Because my brother is a wonderful father. You should have seen how irresponsible he was in his teens. If he can do it, I can, too." He brought his other hand up to her shoulder. "And if you're still worried after a couple of days, we can get a nanny. We'll need one when you go back to work anyway."

She sucked in a breath. "A nanny. I hadn't even thought

about after I go back to work."

"We'll figure it out after we're home." He picked up the seat and wrapped his arm around her shoulders, guided her forward.

They entered the elevator, exited on the sixth floor, and headed down the hall, stopping at the door for the regular nursery. Blaine had been moved there three days before.

Alice smile and opened the door. "Big day for all of you. Let me check your bands."

Although they'd become familiar faces, she gave a perfunctory inspection of all three bands to make sure they matched.

Jasmine found the insulated bag in her carry-all. "I expressed milk last night and this morning. I thought you could use it here." Most of Blaine's meals those first few days had been donated breast milk, and she wanted to help someone else.

Alice took the bag, pulled out the two small bottles, and handed the bag back to Jasmine. "Thank you. We really appreciate this." She wrote on the labels then stuck the bottles into a freezer.

Alice grabbed a diaper from under Blaine's bed. "Let's get him changed and weighed, then you can feed him."

Every time Jasmine had fed him, a nurse weighed Blaine before and after the feeding to make sure he was getting enough milk. One last time.

She sat in her favorite of the two rockers. A low wall separated it from the rest of the nursery. Alice handed Blaine to her, and she prepared to feed him. She was no longer awkward doing it. The first few times, she'd been afraid she'd drop him or hold him too tight.

Nick unbuttoned his shirt, picked up a cloth diaper and tossed it on his shoulder. Whenever he accompanied her, he burped Blaine. It was no longer necessary for him to do the skin-to-skin contact, but she wasn't going to tell him. Blaine could regulate his own body temperature now and had plenty of contact with her while nursing, but she thought Nick enjoyed the bonding time. And the nurses swooned as much as she did.

Feeding time over, Alice weighed Blaine and noted it on his chart.

Right on cue, Dr. Owen, the staff pediatrician, came in. "Let's see if this little guy is ready to go home."

He took Blaine and laid him on a small tissue paper-covered exam table.

Jasmine gave Nick a worried glance. The day before, it had sounded like a sure thing, but now it seemed dependent on something. Nick finished buttoning his shirt and took her hand. Leaning into her, he whispered in her ear. "He's fine."

The doctor picked up the baby and turned around. "You're good to go. Congratulations." He handed Blaine to Jasmine.

Nick stuck out his hand. "Thanks for everything, Dr. Owen. He wouldn't have made it without you."

The doctor peeled off his gloves and shook Nick's hand. "You're welcome. The best part of my job is when I see a baby go home."

After he left, Jasmine placed Blaine on the table and pulled a tiny outfit from her carry-all. She'd purchased several preemie sets, but didn't think he'd wear them for long. She slid one arm into a small sleeve, but she was afraid to bend his other to get it in.

Nick placed his hand on Blaine's belly. "Here, let me."

She stepped sideways. In seconds, Nick had the outfit on the baby.

"How did you do that?"

He plucked a baby blanket from the bag and wrapped Blaine, then lifted him into his arms. "I have a four-year-old niece I visited just after she was born, and my nephew was three months old when we visited my parents for the Fourth of July."

"I'd forgotten you mentioned that. A hands-on uncle, huh?"

He touched foreheads with her. "I was practicing."

Alice carried the baby seat toward them. "Let's get you instructed in this, then you can go." She set the seat on the exam table and took Blaine from Nick. She explained, and demonstrated how to adjust straps and keep the baby safe in the seat.

She stepped back. "There you go. Dad should carry the carseat since you're still healing, Jasmine."

Jasmine hugged the nurse. "Thank you for everything. You and the rest of the nurses made this so much easier than it could have been."

"It was a pleasure having you."

~~~

Nick ticked his fingers on the steering wheel as he waited for a light to change. Traffic was heavier than it had been earlier. "I forgot to tell you. I was late coming down this morning because I was talking to Mom. They're all set to come for the wedding a week from tomorrow."

Jasmine smiled and squeezed his leg. "I can't wait to meet them. How long are they going to stay?"

"Rob and Ruth will be here for four days. Mom, Dad and Tricia are staying six days."

They didn't want to interfere with a honeymoon. He hadn't been able to convince them that with a newborn, there would be no honeymoon. Added to that, no sex yet, and a honeymoon was in the distant future. But he didn't care. The most important thing was Jasmine would be his wife in just over a week. He covered her hand with his.

Three days before, Jasmine had gone shopping for a wedding dress with Anna. Jasmine had insisted she only had the time and energy for one store, and had pored over ads until finding one that seemed to have the widest selection. She was pleased with her dress and had hidden it somewhere in the house before he'd gotten home. Anna had also found her maid-of-honor dress.

He turned into the driveway and parked beside a blue RAV4. "Do you know who that belongs to?"

She frowned. "No."

He tensed. He wouldn't expose his family to any unwanted attention. "Stay here. Lock the doors. I'll go check it out."

He got out and waited until the doors locked before heading to the house. He stepped inside, listening for any unusual sounds. The leather couch in the living room squeaked. He headed there. "Josh! Who owns the RAV4?"

Josh jumped, as if startled, and gripped his hand to his chest. "Oh, man, you scared me. Is Jasmine with you?"

"She's in the car. We didn't recognize the car, so I'm checking it out."

Josh nodded. "Good plan. It's safe to bring her in. My car's been totaled, so that's a rental."

Nick narrowed his eyes and shrugged then headed back outside. He clicked the locks on the car doors, then opened Jasmine's and the back door. "It's Josh. The RAV's a rental since he had an accident with his." He pushed the release on the carseat and straightened up with the seat in his hand.

"What? Is he all right?"

He wrapped an arm around Jasmine. "He looked a little shaky, but otherwise fine." Inside the house, Jasmine sat next to Josh as Nick unbuckled his son and lifted him out of the seat. He settled beside Jasmine.

Josh reached across his sister and touched the sleeping baby's cheek. "Welcome home, little guy."

Jasmine nudged her brother. "Josh, what's going on? Where's your car?"

Josh let out a long breath. "I had an accident. Hey, can I hold the baby?"

Blaine passed from Nick to Jasmine. "Are you sure you're all right?"

Josh awkwardly took the baby into his arms. "I'm fine. Not a scratch." He touched Blaine's cheek and grinned. "Nice to meet you, Blaine. I'm your Uncle Josh. You won't believe the fun we'll have."

Nick chuckled, remembering the fun trouble he'd gotten into with his Uncle Samuel.

Josh leaned back and grinned. "Guess who's coming to the wedding as my guest?"

Jasmine frowned. "No idea."

"Frankie Carlisle."

"Who's—" Her eyes widened. "The detective?"

"Yes."

Nick pulled Jasmine close and kissed her temple. She melted against him. He didn't care who came to the wedding as long as he got to marry the woman he loved.

THE END

Books by Deborah Wallace

Wounded Warrior Hearts Series (Clean Romance)
Wounded Warrior Hearts: Steven
Wounded Warrior Hearts: Amy
Wounded Warrior Hearts: Russ

Rawlins Series (Paranormal Romance – witches)
Kathleen's Legacy
Jason's Forbidden Woman
Jamie's Trials
Adam's Redemption
Kristy's Puzzle

Choice Series (Romantic Suspense)
Second Choice
Third Choice – *Fall 2020*
No Choice – *Winter 2021*

Other Books (Romantic Suspense)
I Shot the Sheriff
New Memories
Father Unknown
Your Love Belongs to Me

Check out my website for details on these books and where to find them. You can also sign up to receive emails when I have a new book. www.DeborahWallaceBooks.com.

Or find my books on Amazon:
amazon.com/Deborah-Wallace/e/B07XDL4X89

Thanks for reading. While you're waiting on the next story, if you would be so kind as to leave a review for this book, that would be wonderful. I appreciate the feedback and support. Reviews lift my spirits and boost my creativity. Thank!

About Deborah Wallace

Someone suggested I try writing, and stories started populating my brain, begging to be put on paper (or my computer screen).

I've got quite a number of books under my belt, but the ones I keep coming back to are the romantic suspense. When I wrote the first *Rawlins* book, I thought it would be the only paranormal. Then I said 'what if…' and now children of the first characters and a couple of friends have books.

I have been called a Jane-of-all-trades, from seamstress to house and furniture designer/builder to computer programmer to technical writer and bookkeeper. I even do car maintenance. I've also guided a team of 'Future Problem Solvers'.

I grew up in Michigan, but Massachusetts has been my home for more years than I care to think about. I love the history here, the museums and antique houses, the seacoast and hiking trails.

My three children have grown and scattered, but my husband is by my side, encouraging my writing.

www.ingramcontent.com/pod-product-compliance
Lightning Source LLC
Chambersburg PA
CBHW030331180626
46810CB00003B/1315